TOASTER POND

Kerri,
Thank you for the opportunity to
do my first book signing at Barnes
and Noble. *Peter de Witt*

BY
PETER DE WITT

DNA Press™
©2006 DNA Press, LLC

TOASTER POND
©2006 by Peter de Witt
©2006 by DNA Press, LLC. All rights reserved.

Library of Congress Cataloging-in-Publication Data

De Witt, Peter, 1970-
    Toaster Pond / Peter de Witt.— 1st ed.
    p. cm.
    Summary: Thirteen-year-old Doug and his two best friends are mysteriously transported through Toaster Pond to a magical place where their unique gifts are needed in a hide-and-seek competition that is much more than a game.

ISBN 1-933255-21-8

[1. Magic—Fiction. 2. Hide-and-seek—Fiction. 3. Contests—Fiction. 4. Best friends—Fiction. 5. Friendship—Fiction. 6. Boarding schools—Fiction. 7. Schools—Fiction.] I. Title.
    PZ7.D532Toa 2006
    [Fic]—dc22

                2 0 0 5 0 2 5 3 6 2

DNA Press, LLC
P.O. BOX 572
Eagleville, PA 19408, USA
www.dnapress.com
editors@dnapress.com

Publisher: DNA Press, LLC
Executive Editor: Alexander Kuklin
Art Direction: Alex Nartea (www.studionvision.com)
Cover Art: Mark Stefanowicz (www.markstef.com)

Doug, Mom, Trish, Jody, Frank & Dawn...
And to Dad...keeping watch from Sanger Castle

Hassan, Pam, Wayne, Frank (3), Seth,
Ashleigh, Brooke, Ali, Mustafa, Khalil

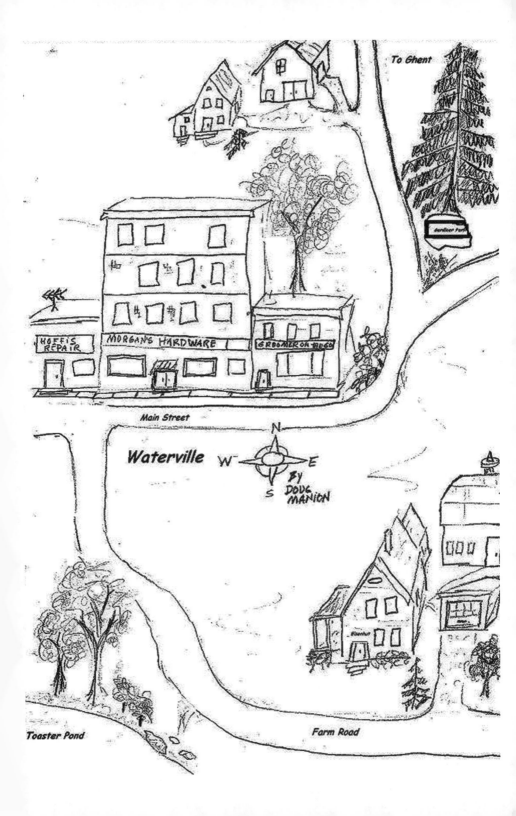

Table of Contents

Thirteen is a magical number. It's often referred to as unlucky.

It brings out strange feelings in many people, and they become paralyzed with fear on days like Friday the 13th. They thank the Heavens that the year is only twelve months long.

Many buildings are designed without a thirteenth floor and streets without a house number thirteen. Silly perhaps... if you're not superstitious.

However, when you're twelve years old, thirteen is a wonderful number. It means you leave your childhood behind and become a teenager. It is a rite of passage into a more mature way of being. As much as becoming a teenager helps you gain maturity into the eyes of people around you it still entitles you to being a child. Yes, being thirteen is a wonderful age. Even more so if you enter Toaster Pond, Sanger Castle, and Shadow Forest, because it allows you entrance into a place too old and scary for young children, and a place forbidden to ordinary adults.

PART I WATERVILLE

Chapter 1.0   Waterville

Long ago there were three prominent families in the small farm town of Waterville. Prominent meaning well to do or wealthy, and as many said they all came from good stock. It sounds like cattle but it was just the way residents described the wealthier residents in town, often with a jealous air.

The Sanger's, Eisenhut's, and Zwevil's were by far the wealthiest families in Waterville. They were actually wealthier than anyone in the neighboring towns of Queensbury and Ghent. However, two of the three couples were the nicest folks you could ever meet. Those two were the Eisenhut's and Sanger's. The third couple, the Zwevil's always felt a little left out and enjoyed making others feel left out as well. The persecuted became the persecutors. It was all very Puritanical.

Through the years, all three families had families. New babies were born and eventually the elder Patriarchs and Matriarchs died off. Although the three families didn't always get along, they shared something that many other families didn't share. They had a "gift." Ordinary people couldn't even begin to comprehend the gift, they had no idea it existed. It was a bond that held each new member of the three families together, whether they liked it or not.

The Zwevil's, Sanger's, and Eisenhut's would meet at the local pub, The Squealing Pig on Friday nights and discuss their dreams of a better life, where they wouldn't have to hide their gift from everyone around them. Waterville was a more exceptional town than most, and all of the families knew that. Many gifted people inhabited the small town but there were many ordinary folks as well. Too many ordinary folks to feel comfortable.

The fifth generation Eisenhut's had a son named Henry and wanted him to experience his gift without the ridicule and hardship that would come with it in average towns. They wanted a place for him to evolve. After all, life is about evolving.

The Eisenhut's and Sanger's knew of a castle where Henry Eisenhut could live life openly when he reached adulthood, tucked away in the Adirondack Mountains, behind Oriskany Falls. A complicated drive for most people but the Eisenhut's and Sanger's never had to travel far, because they had a uniquely quick way of transportation. Which didn't involve the family sedan. It made for fewer miles on their Buick Riviera.

One night after too many brews at the "Pig", Horatio Sanger and Vernon Eisenhut got their nerve up and told Mustafa Zwevil about a place they could go where they could practice their gift openly. Mustafa was excited about the prospect of this tucked away piece of Utopia. After a few days of discussions, Horatio and Virginia Sanger, Effie and Vernon Eisenhut, and Mustafa and Lucinda Zwevil packed some belongings to go on a trip. Effie and Vernon left their small son Henry with their nanny, Pamela Holman; someone they knew could be trusted.

The three couples found their way to the secret portal to the new land.

At Midnight, on a random summer evening, they placed their belongings on the sand and entered Toaster Pond. It sat across Farm Road from the Eisenhut estate. In unison, they stepped into the pond and began wading through the water. Rising up to their knees, then their waists, to their chests, the couples found themselves in over their heads, quite literally, where they sunk down. Toaster Pond always seemed magical, and kids told stories that it was a place where people would throw their old toasters when they drove by, but no one really believed it, because no matter how deep kids dove, a toaster never came into sight. But the name stuck. Nicknames have a way of doing that, even under the oddest of conditions. Not even the most imaginative children in Waterville could have guessed Toaster Pond's true secrets. The Eisenhut's and Sanger's preferred that children thought it was a dumping ground, instead of a magical body of water.

The three families let the water rush over them. However, the Zwevil's were the only ones who had never experienced the trip before. It was fast, peaceful, and painless. The way all trips should be. Twenty feet down to the bottom of the supposed eight-foot deep pond, they floated back up to the surface. It all felt very anticlimactic. Only when they rose to the surface they arrived in Sangerfield, not Waterville where they began their trip. Tucked away past Mount Marcy, Algonquin and Buck Mountains, the land was somewhat surreal, natural and untouched by ordinary humans.

The land was typical mountain land in the Adirondacks, which surprised the Zwevil's. It didn't look special. It was a vast field of grass and a dark forest of trees. Surprisingly, the belongings they left on the sand in Waterville, were waiting for them in Sangerfield. No lost luggage to report, no baggage claims to file.

After walking through a small field, they came upon a hill, and followed a well-marked trail, a large open field, to a hill, which led to Oriskany Falls. The mountain views were behind them and a whole new world ahead of them.

After making it past the falls, an enormous castle was laid out before them. It was a beautiful sight in the midst of a mountainous landscape. However, the beauty was a bit lost on one of the families. After reaching and entering the castle, the Zwevil's became enraged at the fact that they were never told about the land. After all, the three families thought they had no secrets from one another. Or did they?

Unbeknownst to the Sanger's and Eisenhut's, the Zwevil's had an evil side. A true evil side in every sense of the word. The gift they all shared goes two ways, and the Zwevil's chose the dark way. They believed the castle would make the perfect setting for that darkness.

An argument suddenly without reason escalated between Horatio Sanger and Mustafa Zwevil. After many vulgar words thrown by Mustafa, Horatio found himself backed against a wall, quite literally.

"I challenge you to a dual," Horatio said as the wind outside began to pick up and blow wildly.

"A duel," Mustafa scoffed.

"Yes, a duel of wands," Horatio yelled in anger.

Their wives stood back crying, and Vernon Eisenhut felt frozen in fear. "Stop you two. There's enough here for all of us," Eisenhut said trying to convince the two men that fighting wasn't necessary.

"On guard," Horatio said, his wand appearing in his hand. No time to talk it out.

"On guard," Mustafa said in return.

The two men threw a curse at each other. Knowing it would only take one.

"Vado aboleo," screamed Zwevil.

"Vado abolesco," yelled Sanger at the same moment. Both men wanted to destroy each other. Anger clouded their common sense. De-escalation was futile.

Both men had fire in their eyes. Years of fighting and backstabbing came to a head and enveloped both men. Passive aggressive no more, their anger took over. An enormous bolt of lightening crackled through the air striking them dead. Twenty feet apart, they lay still and silent. Dreadful looks frozen on both of their faces.

Effie, Virginia, Vernon and Lucinda stood in disbelief. The silence was deafening. Everything happened so quickly; no one knew what to do.

As the four adults stood looking at the two dead men on the cold hard ground, Lucinda's anger took over her whole body. Although the two men responsible for the fight were both dead, she needed an outlet for her anger. There was a need for someone to blame.

"One day you'll pay for this," Lucinda screamed, and stormed out of the castle toward the forest. She was never heard of again, but her darkness was felt throughout Sangerfield. And she never went back to her home in Waterville.

Rumors spread through the forest among the animals and creatures that inhabited the strange land. The rumor was that Lucinda had twins, and they lived in a castle, which was built in a deep cave. It provided the darkness they needed. Their time spent in the cave gave them a place for their anger to grow. Years of holding in their evilness gave way to a desire to take over Sangerfield.

One day trying to enter the forest with his teenage son Henry to make peace, Vernon found that he was not allowed to enter at all. A spell was cast, and a gift of a different sort spread through the forest. It was a darker gift, which was just as old, but twice as deadly. A power struggle ensued, and there was no end in sight.

Vernon, Virginia, Effie and teenaged Henry made their way back to Waterville, and made frequent visits to Sangerfield. They often brought Henry with them so he could explore the castle. Never once seeing Lucinda or her young twins. However, there were times when the families felt as if they were being followed. The dark crows flying overhead only added to their suspicions that Lucinda and her twins were planning their revenge. Vernon knew that one day he would have to guard his castle, much like Horatio guarded his wife. He only hoped he wouldn't meet the same fate. Survival was his only goal, although he wanted more for Sangerfield and Sanger Castle.

A few years later, Lucinda passed away quietly, but the anger carried on with Ludicrous, and her twin brother Luscious. They were both thirteen when their mother died. Both children vowed to make the Eisenhuts and Sangers pay for the devastation they felt.

Chapter 1.1
Hide-and-Seek

"Ali, Ali in come free," Doug Manion yelled from the base of the robust, dark pine tree in Gardner Park. It was a particularly dark Tuesday evening. The scent of the tree bark passed by his nose. No one came. Doug stared at the chrysalis on the branch hanging in front of him, preparing to yell again.

"Shhh, it's a trick. He's not saying it right," Doug heard a girl's voice, but looked around and didn't see anyone.

"Ali, Ali in come free," he yelled again, voice cracking from the untimely crisp Summer evening air filling his lungs, and the eerie feeling of being all alone. All eyes on him, but he couldn't see anyone.

"No, not yet. I'm waiting until someone else runs in first," a boy's voice said out of the air. Doug looked around, but didn't see anyone again. No sign of any friends running toward safety in the middle of the park. Doug's inner voices had been getting louder over the past couple of weeks. Tonight they seemed to be screaming.

No one ever wanted to be the first one in to touch safety during Hide-and-Seek, just in case they misheard Doug's call of freedom.

The stoic Pine Tree with the stiff bark, looked like it would come alive at any time and pull the average sized Manion up toward the sky, too high for any of his friends to free him from it's clutches.

"You're reading too many horror stories," Doug thought to himself.

Paranoid thoughts began to spiral and freak Doug out a bit. Hearing voices of children who weren't there wasn't helping him much either.

"Couldn't find us," squeaked a female voice.

"Ahh," Doug yelled when he heard it.

"You are such a wimp, Manion," remarked Doug's cousin Skip Corbin. Doug was a little embarrassed that he jumped so high at the sound of her voice.

"No I'm not…Corbin," he answered back mocking his cousin. Hardly sure he sounded believable. Eyeing the tall tree just to make sure the branches weren't moving his way. The tiny bristles on the pine tree seemed to point toward him, just as the tiny hairs on the back of his neck began to stand up. A cool summer breeze blew by his face, and a chill swept over him. Skip looked like she felt it too, but didn't want to admit it. Being the only girl in a group of three best friends was hard enough; she didn't want to portray the squeamish girl as well. That wasn't Skip's style. A farm girl, and a tough one at that, no matter what her five foot two frame portrayed. She stood even height with Doug.

"What's up with the Ali, Ali? It's supposed to Ollie, Ollie oxen free," Skip remarked correcting her cousin.

"I don't know. I felt like saying Ali," Doug said, not really knowing why he changed the call of freedom.

"Well, you better not do that again or Chevy will disqualify you," Skip said.

Doug felt scattered. He wasn't entirely sure why he suddenly changed the call and he was also wasn't sure why he felt so scared to be alone by the tree.

Before trying to convince Skip and himself that he wasn't afraid of the gloomy darkness that was beginning to cover Gardner Park, droves of children began running in from their secret spots. Doug's confidence began to build.

Lauren and Andrea Cowen, sisters, with two years and two inches between them, came running toward the two cousins.

Jaime and Jeff Thompson and Karen Smith, ran from the bushes that stood about thirty yards from Doug. A fleeting thought flew through Doug's mind that the three friends from the bushes saw him eyeing the pine tree. The pine tree that looked considerably smaller now that his peers surrounded him.

"Maybe those were the voices I heard," Doug said to himself, conflicted about whether he heard the whispering of four children from thirty yards away, or voices from inside his head.

"What did you say?" Skip asked.

"Nothing," Doug lied.

Skip gave Doug an odd look as if she really did hear what he said, but wanted him to repeat it for safety's sake.

Wayne Viele, Chuck Mathis and Maggie Doyle began to run out from the trail that led to the running path for the Waterville Cross Country Team, as Dana Degregorio and Laurie Sweet gained momentum behind them. All the teenagers wore wide smiles knowing that they made it to safely to safety.

The very tall Don Frament, a teenage friend from around the corner of Doug's house came running with Janet Sullivan, who was about half of his size. Doug felt a little silly that he couldn't find such big people in such little spots. And there were so many kids playing the game, he couldn't believe that he couldn't find just one kid hiding. Something was blocking his concentration.

However, the kids in Waterville were very good at hiding. It was more than a game, Hide-and-Seek was a sport. Sometimes they played individually, other times they played in teams of two or three.

Within a few minutes, everyone began to run from their hidding spots from around the park.

"We need a blow horn next time," Skip remarked. Doug liked the sound of that.

As soon as Jason Chevrier ran toward the crowd of children with Kim Suedkamp, Lori Habernig, and Michelle Deguire, Doug knew that all of the twenty or so players were together again.

Intimidating because of his size, Jason liked to be the last one in. They called him the sweeper, because he made sure everyone followed the rules and touched safety when they were supposed to. Jason was fourteen, stood nearly six feet tall, looked like a line backer, and was often mistaken for being much older.

It was pretty obvious from the looks of the three girls with him that Jason caught them trying to cheat. Deguire was always sneaky, and tried to get away with breaking a rule or two.

Looking around at the crowd, Doug was hoping that his best friend, Pierce Butterworth, who was running in last, was going to back him up when he made his next suggestion. Of course, he had selfish reasons for making it.

"How about team Hide-and-Seek," Doug said meekly to the rest of the kids.

"No way. We always do that," Pierce piped in first. Other kids grumbled at the thought. Doug knew he was pretty much sunk after that.

"Come on Manion, we always play team," Jason argued.

"Let's play one more game of individual before we have to go home," Skip suggested, knowing that their nine o'clock curfew was quickly approaching. The rest of the crowd agreed with her.

"All right, but we have our last tournament in a couple of days," Doug said, knowing he was going to have to play this next game alone. Staring at the intimidating pine tree, Doug began to count to twenty, not knowing that when he got home, he would be finding out the saddest news he had ever heard in his young life. Not knowing that his life would soon be changing forever.

"One… two… three…" he began counting methodically as everyone snuck away to hide in their crevices for another game of Hide-and-Seek.

"Let's hide behind the bushes over there," a girl's voice whispered. Doug stopped counting and peeked out, but no one was within sight. The cool wind began to pick up and blow the branches above Doug's head. Bristles staring his way again.

"Ready or not, here I come," Doug yelled, and then stopped to listen once more.

"Right here, under the bridge," Jason whispered. Which was odd, because the bridge was about 200 yards away, and yet Doug could hear Jason whispering. It was like Doug had a sixth sense for Hide-and-Seek. And his inner voices were actual people who were speaking. Life was getting odd.

Chapter 1.2
Time to Pass On...

The following night in Waterville was much different, both because of the weather, and the circumstances.

"Severe thunderstorm warning for the residents of Waterville tonight," warned the voice of the weatherman from the antique Crosley Radio.

Ethel Eisenhut was completing various tasks in her chef's kitchen. Not that Mrs. Eisenhut was a chef, but that's what they called the kitchen because of its size. A large island in the middle to prepare food, pots and pans hanging from the ceiling above it. Seemed funny to have such a large kitchen for two people, which only ended up being one on most nights. The pots were never really used for cooking, more for show. Ethel had a way of preparing dinner without turning on her stainless steel oven. A wand was all she needed. Not a spatula or a spoon.

Clearly, the weatherman's forecast was a little behind the speed of the weather. The lightning brightened the night summer sky, and the thunder made the ground and everything on it shake. The windows trembled, and the knickknacks on the mantle moved to the right. More lightning and thunder exploded through the sky, and the knickknacks moved back to the left. It looked as if the figurines of fairies and unicorns were dancing atop the fireplace. The little dance was the gifted version of the Nutcracker Suite.

"It should be passing through there within an hour or so." the weatherman assured the listeners. The listeners in Waterville, however, were not feeling very assured.

More thunder roared through the sky, and a lightening bolt flared over Toaster Pond across the road. Mrs. Eisenhut rolled her eyes. Rufus Eisenhut the 2nd laid under the kitchen table. Rufus wasn't human; he was treated much better than that.

"I could have told him that about a half an hour ago. Not for nothing, but that Frank Holman is just about the right amount of dumb," she said irritated.

Ethel didn't have the patience for mistakes today. Her anxiety overwhelmed her a bit. "That's what he gets for leaving Waterville to be a weatherman, he had the gift," She continued to complain uncontrollably, as if her husband Henry should have been listening, and as if the stress of the night, was completely the weatherman's fault.

Frank escaped to Lyndon College in Vermont because he needed his space from Waterville and his gift. Although his gift as a weatherman was bit off at the moment.

Ethel was a little irritable because she wasn't happy about the storm. It came as such a surprise, and Ethel no longer enjoyed those kinds of surprises

"Yup, sure I can," Henry answered back toward his wife. The statement made no sense at all, and Ethel knew Henry wasn't paying attention.

"You didn't even hear me," Ethel said accusingly.

"I'm sorry," Henry said fixing his imaginary hearing aid as if it was the problem for not hearing his wife. Henry knew that Ethel knew he wasn't paying attention. It was a predicament he didn't enjoy being in.

"Selective hearing, Mr. Eisenhut, is not the fault of your imaginary hearing aid," Mrs. Eisenhut glared with a slight grin.

Henry knew he was off the hook then and there. Ethel only smiled like that when she couldn't hold a grudge against her husband. And how could she hold a grudge anyway, he was leaving to go "out of town," again. Ethel decided not to let her anxiety take precedence over Henry's worries. It would be too selfish of her to do that, and Ethel isn't selfish. The Eisenhut men always had a gift for finding even-tempered women.

The storm outside was worsening. The thunder and lightening were closer together, which meant that Waterville was in the eye of the storm.

Waterville softly held 1,500 people and was quietly tucked in between other towns that were just as small. Queensbury was a small town on the West side and Ghent was to the East. Clinton Corners was to the North and Locust Valley to the South.

Not a big town, Waterville only covered about fifty square miles. Most of those miles were made up of dairy and chicken farms. It was without big businesses and no major attractions. Except, of course, Main Street, which was the major attraction for the residents.

Main Street had numerous stores on it. Numerous meaning five stores actually. Morgan's Hardware, Hoffis T.V. Repair, Sophia's Pizza, Acey's Collectables, and down the street was Degregorio's General Store. The highly successful, Groomer on the Go, was about a mile down Main Street, for those people who loved their pets as much as they loved their children. And there were plenty of those. Ethel Eisenhut was one of them.

All of the stores had been on Main Street in Waterville for years and years, which was just the way the townspeople liked it.

There were a few big houses in Waterville without any farmland, and one of those houses belonged to Henry and Ethel Eisenhut, although it was only Ethel who lived there. Some people referred to their house as an estate because of its size and stature.

Ethel and Henry had pictures from when Henry's parents had a majority of Waterville's land. It was left to them in the Sanger's will. But his parents sold it off when they found themselves spending more time at Sanger Castle.

"I thought it was supposed to be a full Moon tonight," Henry asked.

"It was, but this thunderstorm came out of nowhere," Ethel answered back as she was tuning a new station into the radio, still annoyed by the unfortunate late announcement by Frank Holman.

"Makes me think we should wait until tomorrow morning to go," Henry suggested. Ethel frowned a bit.

"You know you have to travel tonight, so you can be there for the introductions in the morning," she said convincingly. "…And the competition is only a few days away, and you need to be prepared." That was the last Ethel would discuss it.

Henry agreed with her, but still continued to pace around the room doing various activities; like fixing his perfectly trimmed goatee in the mirror and positioning the picture frame that was already centered on the mantle of the fireplace.

"Besides, you know Ludicrous is gearing up for another invasion," Ethel said with disgust. Henry felt a chill go up his spine at the sound of Ludicrous's name, not to mention the word invasion. He walked across the hardwood floors that flowed through all of the rooms on the first floor, over to his black overnight bag, rubbing the instant headache, he got thinking of Ludicrous Zwevil, thanking whoever was responsible for displacing her brother Luscious, because one Zwevil was enough.

Henry gently set his favorite worn-down sweater on top of the other clothes in the bag, which seemed to disappear inside. Ethel eyeing his every procrastinated move.

"How were the Manion's holding up at the wake tonight," he asked.

"They were all right. Anxious, but all right," she said keeping an eye on the time.

"You have to hurry, Hun, they'll leave without you. You don't want her traveling with them alone. She's a little nervous about being seen," Ethel said rushing Henry as he was zipping up his black leather bag.

"They've been waiting ten minutes, they can wait another five," Henry snapped back, then paused, and gave a little sigh.

"I'm sorry Dear, I know she's anxious. I'll leave in a minute," he said sheepishly, not wanting to hurt his wife's feelings.

"I know you hate going without me, but I'll see you in a few days. This competition is more important this year than ever before," Ethel said lecturing her husband. He knew she was right, and began to pick up his pace so he could join his guests outside.

"You be careful on your trip and make her feel comfortable,

please. She's going to be one of the best," Ethel pleaded with her husband as he walked through the hallway one more time.

"You know I will. I'll miss you, my Lady," Henry said kissing her hand as he walked out the door toward the pond.

"I just hope it's not premature to bring her," Henry confided.

"Me too, but I think we need to be positive about all of this," Ethel said to her husband from inside the screen door as she waved to the others waiting to leave.

Henry looked back and yelled, "Are you sure those are the three you want to send?" Knowing the answer already.

Ethel patiently shook her head yes, and said," Definitely, and tomorrow night will only cement that thought."

Henry walked toward the people who were waiting for him, as Ethel watched. The handsome man with dark hair reminded her of Lord Sanger. The short, round female was an old friend of hers, and she wanted to make sure that Henry was overly careful with her, because she seemed to be nervous about the trip, but also a little sad to be leaving. It had been a hard day for the woman and her family.

The group with Henry waved to Mrs. Eisenhut to say goodbye before entering Toaster Pond, and Ethel recited her favorite poem. In an instant, they were gone. A bolt of lightening flashed, and a crack of thunder echoed through the sky.

"That was close," Ethel thought to herself. The sound of the storm startled her a bit. She was hoping her husband's trip would be uneventful.

"He's going to have enough to worry about in a few days," she said to Rufus, although Rufus was clearly too worried about the storm to listen to Ethel.

He walked quickly behind the couch from his spot under the table. Ethel rolled her eyes at her cowardly dog.

Ethel stared outside at the thunderous night sky, and walked outside the screen door to the porch. Rufus, her fearless guard dog, whimpered from behind the couch. Thunderstorms were his worst enemy, and this one was the biggest they'd seen in years. Ethel rolled her eyes. She went to sit down on the porch swing to watch nature's entertainment. The dog lumbered behind her knowing that she would keep him safe.

Ethel stared at the small pond across the road from the house. It seemed so magical, especially on a stormy summer night. Lightening seemed to bounce off its surface.

"Let's go Rufus, we have work to do for the new ones," she yelled walking back inside her enormous white house on the corner of Farm Road, across from the magical Toaster Pond. Rufus got up grumbling and walked toward her, all too happy to go back to his safe spot behind the couch.

The Burning Bushes and large sunflowers were blowing left to right in the heavy wind of the storm. Rain drenched the ground. The porch swing began to swing back and forth. There was a strange feeling in the air in Waterville.

Chapter 1.3
Vanishing Act

"Poor little Dear," a wrinkled faced old woman said sadly pinching Doug's cheeks. Doug couldn't believe how much his life had changed in the past twenty-four hours. Last night he was playing a game of Hide-and-Seek with all of his friends from town, and tonight he was at a wake for his favorite grandmother, Corbin Gram, the one who baked Banana Bread and cooked elaborate dinners using various herbs from her secret garden. Oddly, Doug was never allowed in the kitchen to watch her make dinner, and it was always spotless when she was done cooking. She seemed to never make a mess.

Walking in the door the night before, he knew something was wrong. There was an eerie silence as soon as his parents laid eyes on him, staring at him, not knowing what to say. How could two nights be so close together, and yet so drastically different? Life changed so quickly.

As if it weren't bad enough that his favorite grandmother passed away, now his house was filled with unfamiliar people after the wake and an old woman was grabbing at his sun drenched, freckled cheeks. She pinched the right side and then the left, and then pinched both sides together. It was not making for a good night at the Manion household. Doug needed his space. No inner voices had to let him in on that.

The storm outside was getting worse, and every time the thunder boomed, the house shook. People would jump with every crack of lightening, and no one wanted to leave the house until the storm let up, which meant for a long night of talking with people Doug didn't know. The sky had grown dark and the clouds rolled in. A gray blanket of clouds slightly covered the once full moon. It was an eerie addition to the already dismal day.

Corbin Gram passed away suddenly the night before while Doug was mindlessly playing Hide-and-Seek with his friends. She had been a high school Science teacher for 30 years before she retired, and in her spare time she taught night courses in the Science Department at the University of Utica. Doug always liked it when they would see her university students at Sanger Mall. They would call her Professor Corbin, which Doug thought made her sound very sophisticated, he hoped to follow in her footsteps some day. Even at thirteen, which he had just turned a few weeks before, he had the goal of going away to a college or university, and studying…something to do with Science. Not knowing what he was gifted in.

"Big dormitories, with no little sister. No annoyances," he thought to himself whenever his little sister Beck was getting on his nerves. Daydreaming aside, he looked around at all the sad people who inhabited his house. Glancing over to his mother in between pinches, he saw her tearing up all over again. Corbin Gram was her mother, and she used to come to the house every Sunday to get her hair cut by Doug's mother, Marilyn. Then they would cook all day after her haircut was finished. Now, after thirteen years of wonderful Sundays, his favorite grandmother was gone, and he was trying to ignore the woman who had hold of his cheeks.

"Thank you, Ma'am," Doug said and walked away as quickly and as politely as he could from the pinching cheeks lady who had spent the past ten minutes giving Doug's freckled face too much attention.

Searching for a moment's peace from the crowd, he made his way up the stairs to his bedroom, so happy to have a minute by himself. No old people grabbing his face, or unfamiliar people grabbing and hugging him, and no Beck tugging on his shirt, looking up at him, asking for more food, or telling him she's bored. He kind of wished that his cousin Skip didn't leave so early. He could have used her companionship. Safety in numbers from the elderly guests.

Doug lay down on his bed and stared up at the dark ceiling, listening to the loud cracks of thunder making their way slowly across Waterville. He was too solemn to be frightened by the sound, unlike the night before with the stoic pine tree.

"Dhoug," a voice whispered from the empty second floor hallway.

Feeling annoyed, he thought he would never get away from the well wishers from the wake.

"I'm in here," Doug yelled to the anonymous voice, or perhaps the inner voice. It was somehow familiar, but he couldn't quite place it.

"Dhouuugg," more whispering of his name coming closer down the hallway.

"I'm in here," Doug yelled to whatever relative was calling to him.

No one came into his room. Rolling his eyes, he unfolded his arms and began to sit up in his bed. He shuddered to think it could be the wrinkled old woman looking for freshly pinched cheeks. Perhaps answering the voice was a mistake. He was better off hiding, but it was too late for that.

"Dooooug," a voice politely whispered through the hallway for the third time.

"I'm coming," he grumbled.

As he got up to answer whoever was in the hallway, his body became rigid with annoyance, and perhaps a little fear.

"What," he said rudely walking out of his bedroom, looking up into the dark hallway, but no one was there. The hall was completely empty, and it seemed to be getting darker every second. He couldn't figure out who was behind that voice.

Glancing to his left, he saw nothing but an empty hallway that led to his parents bedroom. Then right, and all that was there was a hallway filled with nothing but the staircase downstairs and the doorway to his sister's room. Looking behind him, back into his bedroom, he saw emptiness fill his room.

Then he looked ahead to the wall in front of him. A little chill crawled quickly up his spine. Looking around again, it felt like someone was there, but he was standing on the cold wooden floor all alone. In front of him was a picture of Corbin Gram with the rest of his family. A profound sadness fell over him for a moment, realizing maybe he was hearing an inner voice that he longed to hear, which was the voice of his grandmother.

Running down the hall to look in his sister's room, he wanted to make sure Beck wasn't responsible for the voice. No one was there. Slowly, he knelt down to peek under her bed. Nothing. Not even the voice anymore. Quickly, he stood up and walked over to her closet.

"Beck," he yelled, and opened the double doors, but no one was in there either.

Doug bolted out of Beck's room and looked down the stairs. Empty and vacant, he was standing all alone but hearing more inner voices. Something that was happening all too often lately.

As he walked quickly down the stairs, thunder cracked above the house and lightening lit up the sky. He jumped and nearly fell down the twelve steps that led to the living room. Catching himself before breaking a leg, he ran down the rest of the stairs.

"Hey Big Guy, what's wrong? You look like you've seen a ghost," Doug's Dad said to him when he reached the kitchen.

They both realized that was an untimely phrase to use.

"I'm fine," Doug stuttered a bit, and sat down on the kitchen stool.

"That is so weird," he thought to himself.

"What's weird," his Dad asked.

"Nothing," Doug said, and got up from the stool and began to walk out of the kitchen, annoyed by his inner voices.

Safety in numbers was all he could think, making his way through the door into the living room where the wrinkled old woman who loved to pinch his cheeks was standing. He couldn't decide which was worse, the woman or the noises coming from nowhere upstairs.

"I thought you ran out on me Duggles in the Moonlight," she said in her slow, old, creaking voice.

"I was looking all around for you down here," she said to him. One eye looking at him, the other lazily wandering around the room.

She had two fake eyebrows that were dark black. The one above her right eye was hanging down toward her nose. Doug didn't think it would be polite to fix it for her.

Closing his eyes, Doug wished she would disappear. Feeling totally taken over by the thought, he felt focused, unable to hear any voices at all. It was the first time he felt clarity since playing hide and seek the night before. When he opened his eyes, she was gone. He blinked quickly and looked around. She was still gone.

"Where'd she go? There is no way she could have run away that fast," Doug thought to himself.

He looked around and no one seemed to notice that an annoying old women with a fondness for pinching cheeks had suddenly disappeared. Doug's cheeks began to turn red. Trying not to panic, he scanned the room looking for the woman or at least for a guest who saw the whole incident. No one looked over at him to signify any concern. A tingling sensation consumed his body, and he felt faint. Moments away from passing out, he tried to breathe deeply.

"She's fine. She's home now," was all he began to hear in his head.

Doug wasn't sure if it was an inner voice at work telling him the truth, or if he was just trying to make himself feel better.

"Douglas, I need you in the kitchen," his father said from the kitchen.

Suddenly, Doug came back to reality. His breathing returned to normal, and he felt like he imagined the whole thing, but wasn't sure.

"Doug, in here," his father said a second time.

"I didn't do it on purpose," Doug confessed to his Dad as he walked in the kitchen ready to break into tears.

"What are you talking about," Mr. Manion asked.

"The woman just disappeared," Doug said beginning to panic.

"Calm down Kiddo. What woman," his Dad asked.

"The one who pinched my cheeks," Doug explained.

"You're just a little shocked from everything with Corbin Gram,"

Dad suggested.

Doug kept looking around the room, behind counter tops, trying to make sure she wasn't playing Hide-and-Seek.

"She's good, if she is playing," Doug said to himself.

Doug's Dad continued to stare at Doug wondering what intervention he should try to calm his son down.

"Why don't you go out to the porch to get some air?" Mr. Manion suggested.

Hoping that she would appear again soon, Doug went out for a breather. A second later, a concerned older woman walked into the kitchen.

"Have you seen Anna?" she asked Mr. Manion.

"I haven't seen her for a few hours," he answered looking out to the porch. One eye raised.

Doug took a deep breath, realizing they were talking about the woman he made disappear. Suddenly realizing that he didn't imagine the whole situation. The event really happened. And the fact that no one noticed in a filled room was just as surprising to him. Obviously people were too overcome with grief because of Corbin Gram's passing.

"Hmm. She must have gotten a ride home with someone else," the woman thought out loud with concern and then turned around and left.

Doug looked toward the floor, and his father looked right at him through the screen door. Neither one said a word. Doug had the feeling his father knew exactly what happened, but was too worried to ask.

Chapter 2.0
Strange Behavior

L ater that evening, after everyone left the Manion household, Doug's Dad walked him up their creaky stairs to bed, after Beck went to sleep. Mrs. Manion needed some time alone in her bedroom. Doug looked down the dark hallway and saw that the door was ajar, but not enough to see his mother. He swore he heard her sobbing, but after the events from earlier, he couldn't be certain that he was hearing anything correctly.

Doug was sad to see his Mom so distraught. It almost seemed like she was avoiding her two children, but he tried to understand.

They rounded the corner into his bedroom, and he felt a little better that the lights were on in his room. The lights made him feel safe, as if a voice wouldn't appear if the lights were on.

However, he didn't feel good enough to tell his Dad about the events from earlier in the evening. Perhaps the sadness of losing his grandmother was making him hear voices that weren't there. Figuring out the unseen person responsible for the voice was a job he would do on his own. Other questions lingered that he wanted to clear with his father, and they didn't involve the disappearance of an old woman.

"Dad, is Mom going to be all right?" Doug asked.

"Yeah, Kiddo, she will be. She's just having a tough time right now," his father answered sitting on the bed as Doug got under the covers.

"Uhm," Doug began and then thought better about his next

question. He wanted to choose his words carefully, waiting until his head was securely on the two soft pillows.

"What is it?" his father asked, anticipating that Doug had another question. Doug thought for a moment more.

"Where do you think Gram went when she died?"

Doug knew he was asking his father a deep question, but he was thirteen now and could handle the answer.

"Wow, you're hitting me with the hard questions tonight heh," his father answered back with a smile. A little seriousness in jest.

Anxiety stricken, Doug thought his question was somehow inappropriate, even though the question was about his favorite grandmother.

"We don't have time tonight for the long answer Kiddo. Can I give you the short version?" his father asked with a smile, which made Doug feel better.

"Yeah," Doug agreed.

It was better than no version at all. Mr. Manion seemed to be avoiding the question.

"I can tell you this. I know she's in a better place," his father said looking very sure of himself.

A half-smile formed on Doug's face. That answer was good enough for this evening. His father never lied to him before, so there really wasn't any reason to believe he was lying now. Doug could tell his father was holding the full answer back though. After the anonymous voice from before, and the disappearance of the pinching cheeks lady, Doug decided the long answer was worth waiting for. The pillows and his bed were beginning to feel comfortable, and he decided he was too tired to hear it tonight. The long day was catching up with him. Although he was still a little scared to be alone. He wished his fears would disappear as fast as the elderly woman named Anna. At least he wouldn't feel guilty for making those disappear.

"Goodnight Son," Mr. Manion said, giving Doug a kiss on the forehead, and began to get up from Doug's bed.

"Dad," Doug said quickly. His Father sat back down.

He knew his son didn't want to be alone for some reason.

"Yes," he answered with a sigh.

"Will you tell me that story about playing Hide-and-Seek when you were my age," Doug asked.

There was a pause for a few seconds, deciding whether he wanted to or not, but he couldn't help but think something was wrong with Doug.

"Are you ok?" his dad asked.

"Yeah, I just need to hear a happy story right now," Doug said, sadly trying to get his father to stay.

"Well, your Uncle Bill Corbin and I used to play Hide-and-Seek over by the woods near Toaster Pond with Nancy Simboli and most of the kids from Waterville," Mr. Manion began.

"There aren't any woods near Toaster Pond," Doug interrupted.

His father looked surprised, as if he misspoke and gave too much information.

"Do you want to hear the story or not," his father asked with a grin, feeling a little taken aback.

"Sorry," Doug apologized. "Just one more question," Doug asked slightly.

"What's that," his father answered.

"Where was Pierce's Dad?"

"Duncan didn't move to Waterville until our freshman year in high school," Mr. Manion answered.

"We used to get together, and Bill and I were always on the same team with Nancy. We planned it that way. Anyway, one dark night I was chosen to be the hunter," he explained.

"What's a hunter? You mean seeker Dad," Doug interrupted again, feeling unsatisfied with the story's beginning.

"Oh yeah, the seeker. I'm sorry Doug; I guess I'm not much for stories tonight," his father said distractedly. "Can I get a rain check for this one?" his Dad asked looking a bit conflicted.

"Yeah," Doug said disappointedly.

Mr. Manion got up and turned off the light. Doug rolled over with one pillow underneath his head and another one in his arms. He hugged the soft white pillow that barely had any stuffing left in it, and faced the window to look outside in the newly moonlit sky. If anything was in the hallway earlier, he hoped that it passed through with the thunderstorm.

The storm had passed as quickly as it came, and there was a warm summer breeze flowing tenderly in the window toward Doug. What an odd night it had been. And to top it off, his Dad couldn't finish the Hide-and-Seek story. That was a first. It was Mr. Manion's favorite story.

There was one lone star that shone brightly in the sky as Doug stared through the dark room out his window. The warm air continued to quietly flow into the room. It almost felt like the warm summer air was kissing his cheek, just like Corbin Gram used to on Sunday evenings before she left for home. She always brought him up to bed on Sundays. It was going to be one of the things he missed the most.

Chapter 2.1
Boarding School?

"I'm just going to miss her so much," Doug heard his mother saying when he woke up the next morning. Looking around, he couldn't see his parents in the hallway, but could hear his mother whispering.

She sounded like she was crying, but Doug couldn't tell because she wasn't in sight.

"You have to think that she is in a better place," his father said using the same line on Doug's mom that he used on Doug the night before.

"It's bad enough that she needs to go but now he might go as well," she said.

Doug was a little confused on where his parents' conversation was going, but could hear them as if he was standing right next to them. Just like the voices from the game of Hide-and-Seek, Doug's voices were loud and in tune.

He sat up in bed and tried not to make a sound. Both bedroom doors were closed, and he focused on the conversation quietly taking place in his parents' bedroom down the hall.

"Honey, you have to think of it as a compliment that they're offering Doug this chance," Mr. Manion said trying to convince his wife.

"I know, but I would miss him if he we're gone too," she said weeping.

"Think of it as boarding school, not something dangerous," his father said trying to concentrate on the positive.

"They want to send me to boarding school," Doug thought to himself, feeling as if he did something wrong.

"They didn't even ask me for my opinion."

Feeling angry, he closed his eyes to focus on their voices. Visions of being sent to a military school, waking up at 5 a.m. to do a thousand push-ups every morning was all that came into view.

"Listen, he'll be there with her and it will be like old times," he heard his father say.

"Yeah, but they won't be here," Mrs. Manion replied.

"Who will be with me?" Doug thought, too preoccupied by the announcement that he wasn't supposed to know yet.

"Just think, he will be the first one to ever attend the school for the gifted," his father explained.

"Gifted," Doug thought. "I'm gifted. I mean I do well in Science and stuff, but I'm gifted?"

Suddenly, the disappointment of going to a boarding school conflicted with Doug's happiness to think he was gifted or somehow smarter than everyone in Waterville.

"I told Mr. Sweeney that I was better at Math than he thought," Doug remembered back to the after-school conversation that his Math teacher had with him in the spring.

The conversation between his parents suddenly became mute. He couldn't hear any more voices.

Throughout the morning Doug found himself sulking about the possibility of being sent away, but wanted to know why his parents hadn't told him yet.

"I have good grades, I've never had to go see Mr. Malet, the Principal, and now I'm being sent away." feeling frustrated that he could no longer tune in the conversation that his parents were having.

"Knock, knock," Doug recognized his father's tap on the door.

"Come in," he said depressingly.

"Hey Kiddo," you all right? I haven't seen you all morning," his father asked.

"Maybe you should open your door," Doug thought to himself. Doug wanted to ask him about the conversation, but knew he wasn't supposed to overhear it, so didn't say a word to his Dad.

"Why is the funeral tonight, anyway?" Doug asked trying to change the subject.

"It's a tradition in our families to have the funerals at night," his Dad answered. "We like to wait until it's almost dark."

"Great tradition," Doug mumbled sarcastically.

"Most people have traditions that deal with special dinners or holidays, not funerals," Doug thought to himself.

"What's that," his father asked.

"Nothing," Doug said quietly realizing some of his thoughts were out loud.

"Seriously Doug, are you ok?" his father asked.

"Yeah, I'm fine," Doug lied. "I'll be better tomorrow."

"Are you competing in the big Hide-and-Seek Tournament tonight?" his father asked trying to change the subject.

"Yeah, if you wouldn't mind," Doug said feeling a little more himself as he thought about the tournament. Although, he felt a little guilty playing Hide-and-Seek on the night of his grandmother's funeral, but his father really pushed to make sure his life stayed normal given the circumstances.

"Well, why don't you get dressed. Lots of chores to do in the barn, and then we have to go eat an early dinner and meet at the church around five," his father said.

"Yes, Sir," Doug politely said to his dad. Mr. Manion got up and walked out the door. "Chores. I wish I could make those disappear," he grumbled in the mirror walking over to his closet to get his work clothes.

Chapter 2.2
Ringers

After Corbin Gram's funeral that evening, Doug got permission to take off on his mountain bike to meet up with his cousin Skip and their best friend, Pierce.

"Just wear your reflectors," his father said as Doug walked out the door.

Skip told Doug that she would meet him at Pierce's house. It was a hot Summer Thursday evening, and Doug was thankful to be out of his dress clothes and in shorts and a t-shirt.

After the difficult past few days, he was looking forward to hanging out with Pierce and Skip. Although Doug intended on keeping the boarding school decision to himself.

They were getting prepared to play team Hide-and-Seek. It was a weekly event on Thursday nights during the summer for all of the kids from Waterville. The sun was itself beginning its nightly hiding game, and the moon was rising higher in the sky. Doug was getting excited to get to Pierce's house so they could be on their way to Gardner Park.

Pierce was a few inches taller than Doug, and his jet-black hair and blue eyes were a magnet for all the girls in junior high. Besides looks, Pierce was talented at any sport he played. He was a gifted athlete, but didn't get the grades that his friends did. In seventh grade, Pierce was close to failing, so he was pretty happy to be starting eighth grade in the fall. Academics were not his forte, which was odd, because his father had his PhD in Biology, and until recently was a Professor of Biology at the University of Utica. Recently, because a few weeks ago Pierce's Dad disappeared, and the Waterville Police were not being very helpful in the search. Pierce and his mom were not forthcoming with details.

"Maybe Dr. Butterworth was too stressed out and needed to start a new life somewhere else," Sheriff Cordes whispered. The comment didn't seem to bother Pierce. Doug thought, both the idea of Dr. Butterworth being stressed and Pierce's flippant attitude were both odd.

"If my Dad were missing, I would search 24/7 to find him," Doug thought to himself.

Pierce stayed quiet about the whole situation, even when Doug or Skip tried to prod him into talking about it. The three friends were vastly different, but together made a good team. In the near future they would find out how important that would be.

Skip finally made it to Pierce's house, and made sure that she would be driven home, because it would be too late for her to ride her bike when the game ended. Doug had his overnight bag so he could spend the night at Pierce's. His belongings overflowed out of the bag. Doug always packed heavy.

"How much did you pack?" Pierce said making fun of his best friend's backpack.

"I needed a few things just in case," Doug retorted.

"Just in case what, we get stranded in the woods," Pierce said laughing.

"How did you fit it all in there?" Skip asked.

"It wasn't easy," Doug answered feeling a little annoyed by all of the unwanted attention. He was very modest and didn't like the focus suddenly being on him.

"How's your Dad?" Doug asked.

"About the same as your Mom," Skip said having heard her father weeping over the phone speaking to Doug's mom, Marilyn.

Doug felt a little bad that he was about to go and have fun, knowing his mother was at home upset, but he needed to play Hide-and-Seek for a while to get everything else off his mind. After all, he was being sent away to boarding school in the fall.

"Are you guys ready?" Pierce's mom called from downstairs in the foyer.

Skip shrugged her shoulders to say she was, and Doug nodded trying to pull things out of his stuffed backpack. Pierce knew they needed a little more time.

"Can you give us ten minutes Mom?" Pierce asked.

"Sure, planning the big strategy?" she kidded.

"Actually, not yet, but we need to," Pierce answered looking concerned at his two teammates.

Hide-and-Seek gets pretty serious in Waterville. Gardner Park has some baseball fields but mostly it's a wooded area. The trails flowed through making it perfect for running and walking. Although it was well wooded, the players knew the boundaries.

Pierce took the wrinkled Hide-and-Seek notice out of his dresser drawer. There was an air of seriousness when Pierce read the very formal announcement with a picture of a diamond on it for the proper effect.

Hide-and-Seek Championship
Hunt For the Faux Diamond
Where: Gardner Park
When: Thursday, July 30th
Time: 8:00, 13 &14 year olds
9:00 for 15 & 16 year olds who are interested
Who: Three person teams. Make them up before you come.

Boundaries:
North through the woods to North Marker
(Blue Marker on Big Pine Tree)
South to Baseball Field
West to Sidewalk next to Naylor Drive
East to Main Street Sidewalk
Safety: **Big Ben:** Pine Tree in Center of Park

Positions:
Seeker, Hider, Guard

Rules
Seekers; stand at the tree and slowly count to twenty. Seeker's job is to catch as many hiders as possible. Seekers cannot tag the guards, and they wear a pouch to collect the flags.

Guards; stand around their Pre-chosen prison. Guards are able to leave their prisons to protect their seekers, but if they leave their prisons unattended, other guards can free the captured prisoners already in their possession. Unattended prisoners do not have to stay in prison (So it would be dumb to let them).

Hiders; wear their team flag and hide from the seekers. The Hider's job is to find the hidden Faux Diamond and get it back to safety without getting caught.

First hider to get to safety with the Faux Diamond wins. Any Hider caught by a Seeker in the process will have to give the Faux Diamond to the referee to hide again.

Game ends when the Faux Diamond is found.

Sudden Death: If the Faux Diamond is not found in one hour, the team with the most prisoners captured, wins.

There will be referees, so don't even think about cheating!

"What's our plan?" Skip asked.

"Same as always. You protect our prison and I seek for Hiders. Doug looks for the diamond. When I catch someone, you guard them in solitary," Pierce said.

"Same plan as always," Skip said in agreement, but a little disappointed she wasn't playing a new position.

"Might as well do what works," Doug answered.

"Listen guys," Pierce began.

"And girls," Skip interrupted.

"Listen team," Pierce said with a smile. "We have won most of these games this summer. Let's win the big one and get the diamond," he said sounding as if he needed to rally the troops.

Doug and Skip laughed a bit, considering they were the troops, but deep down inside they wanted to win just as badly as Pierce.

The three teammates ran down the stairs, prepared for battle. Doug was wearing his red and hunter green striped team flag around his waist.

"Are you guys and girl, ready for war?" Mrs. O'Brien-Butterworth asked with a smile.

"Yeah," the three answered back.

Pierce's Mom dropped the three off at Gardner Park, waved goodbye, and yelled,

"I'll pick you up at 9:15."

Pierce gave her the thumbs up. They liked to hang around and watch the older kids play after their game ended, but lately there weren't many older kids showing up.

Doug, Skip, and Pierce began walking across Gardner Park. Dusk was setting in, and they saw the silhouettes of three kids.

"Hey, look who's here. The three losers," a voice said behind Pierce's back. Pierce started to lunge toward the kid who was trying to taunt them.

"Pierce, stop!" Doug yelled.

"He's not worth it," Pierce coolly said to Doug trying to de-escalate his anger.

"I didn't think they allowed twelve year olds to play," said the blonde haired boy who seemed to think his remark was somehow hard hitting.

"Teddy, we're thirteen now," Skip said back defending herself and two friends.

"Wow, are you sure you can stay out at night?" he teased.

Teddy Hemmings was vocal, which had its good and bad points. Skip and Doug were never sure if he liked them or not, but secretly, they didn't much care either way. However, he and Pierce were like oil and water.

Going into eighth grade with them, Teddy wasn't fond of Pierce. Pierce beat him out for Captain of the soccer team last summer. Teddy hung around with two people, and two people only. There were probably a variety of reasons for the limited number. Those two were Brooke Nichols and Bradley Scott. Brooke and Bradley were always pretty quiet. There were a variety of reasons for that as well.

"Keep your mouth shut Hemmings," Pierce said angrily.

"We'll do our talking out on the field," Skip warned. And with that she grabbed Pierce's arm and pulled him away.

"Got a girl talking for you," was the best comment that Teddy could think of as Doug, Skip, and Pierce walked away.

"What is that all about?" Doug asked Pierce as they got out of earshot of Teddy.

"He irritates me," Pierce answered.

"He's not worth fighting," Doug said back.

"I know. But he makes me so mad," Pierce explained back.

They let it go after that and walked toward Big Ben, the pine tree in the center of the park, the same huge tree that scared Doug a few nights earlier. A boy in a long black robe stood next to Big Ben. It was tradition for an older boy to referee the championship Hide-and-Seek game, and they had to be dressed for the part.

Eighteen-year-old Parker Gardner was the boy who would referee the game. Parker's parents financed the building of the fields, and paid for the cleaning and up-keep of the park. Parker's father was a very wealthy lawyer in town, and he also was a long time resident of Waterville. Pierce's mom worked as a lawyer in Mr. Gardner's law firm, so Pierce enjoyed having Parker as the referee.

"You know the rules. I'll be watching out in the park," Parker began, looking rather frightening in his black robe.

"I also have a friend today who is here to watch," Parker explained

pointing to an older girl without ever introducing her.

She was wearing the same type of robe as Parker; only it was black with soft purple lines all through it. Just like a Magic Eye, Doug stared at the robe long enough to realize the purple lines were little triangles. Doug made a note to himself to read about triangles, because he remembered hearing their significance before. Doug was always inquisitive.

Although he had never seen her before, he was happy there was an extra ref just in case Teddy tried to cheat. Doug noticed that the unknown girl was staring at him. She made a point to look away every time Doug looked over. It began to give him the creeps.

"All right, I set the time for ONE half hour. Listen for the blow horn at half-time. You will have five minutes to rest, and then I'll blow the horn again to start the second half. At the fourth sound of the horn, the game will be over. The team with the Faux Diamond, wins the championship. All teams should have come earlier today to designate a spot for their prison. The team that wins today will receive the Hide-and-Seek trophy," Parker said.

With the sound of the blow horn, the teams took off. All Seekers were held in the middle of the field to count for twenty seconds.

"GO!" Parker yelled, and the Seekers took off in separate directions to find the hiders.

Teddy was not very happy because Pierce beat him into the woods, which is the way it usually played out every game.

Pierce ran into the woods and noticed a shadow in his peripheral vision. Slowly he turned, and his feet lifted above the leaves. Floating through the air just above the leaves, he dove after the hider, and grabbed her flag. It was Brooke Nichols.

"How did you do that," Brooke asked Pierce.

"How'd I do what," Pierce said coyly.

"I didn't even hear you," Brooke said in disbelief.

"I'm that good," Pierce said with a smile trying to hide his true talent.

Brooke walked off toward the park to go to Skip's prison. There was no sense in cheating because Pierce held Brooke's team flag in his black pouch.

Pierce hadn't shared his floating talent with Skip or Doug yet. He had a few other secrets too. New things began happening to him when he turned thirteen, and he wasn't sure how much he could share with his two best friends yet.

Doug began looking around the trees in the wooded section of the park.

"Shhh, I see someone moving up there," a voice said.

Doug turned around, but couldn't see anyone.

"Look, he's over there," Doug heard Teddy say to Bradley Scott.

Brad was clearly away from his prison, trying to help Teddy find the diamond. Doug could hear their voices like they were close by, but they were whispering, and he realized the inner voices were working for him. Doug could see their silhouettes moving about one hundred yards away.

Crouching down by a tree, Doug closed his eyes and began rubbing the new necklace his father gave him for his birthday. Trying to hide, he crouched down as far as he could. Footsteps came closer and stepped right next to him. Doug was sure he was about to be caught. Letting his fear go, he wished he could disappear. Feeling very focused, Doug stayed silent to see if Bradley and Teddy would walk by, which they did. Practically stepping on Doug's foot, they quietly walked by, over fragile leaves that broke under their feet.

"I thought he was right here," Teddy said to Bradley.

"He was. Where'd he go?" Bradley asked looking really confused.

Doug looked up and noticed Bradley was looking right at him. Ready to say something to Teddy, Doug began to stand up, but noticed that Teddy was staring his way as well. Neither one of them could see Doug.

Doug looked down at his wrist to see how much time he had left in the game, and couldn't see his wrist either.

"I'm invisible," Doug said to himself.

Teddy and Bradley walked away, never hearing a thing.

"That's so weird. He was right there," Teddy said feeling irritated.

Doug grabbed his necklace and rubbed it. Suddenly, he reappeared. The sound of the blow horn echoed through the woods. He sat down; feeling stunned, and took a breather.

"I can hear people when they're talking about me from far away, my necklace makes me invisible, and I can make old ladies disappear." Even Doug had to admit this was odd.

It was all too much for Doug. As surprised as he was, he realized that it helped him with his game of Hide-and-Seek. At least there was a positive side.

The blow horn blew one more time, and Doug stood up and began looking for the Faux Diamond. The hardest part was finding the six-inch fake diamond in the middle of the woods.

"A needle in a haystack would be easier than this," Doug thought.

As Doug was searching for the diamond, Pierce was grabbing people left and right in another part of the woods. He hovered across the ground, making absolutely no noise. Skip, in the clearing of the park, realized that she was guarding about ten prisoners, and had no desire to see them go free. Confident that her teammates were doing their part, she stayed near her prison, making sure none of the hiders tried to run and get new flags from their home base.

Doug found himself searching through the dark woods for the diamond. Ducking out of the way every time he heard voices, he looked over toward the wooden bridge. It crossed the stream that went through Gardner Park. Near the bridge shone a large rock, which was actually the diamond.

"I have no idea where to look," a voice said walking by Doug as he hid behind a tree. The person walked right over the bridge and didn't see the very thing they were looking for.

"Looking too hard. Can't see it in front of them," Doug said to himself.

He was hoping they were not going to turn around, because the diamond would have come into view. Slowly he walked over and grabbed the Faux Diamond. A chill fell over his body, knowing he was very close to winning the championship. Holding the diamond in his left hand, Doug began making a path through the tall grass and trees that filled the park. Conflicted whether he should give his necklace a spin and make his invisible way to safety he instead opted for good sportsmanship and left his necklace alone.

Stopping near the clearing where the woods ended and the field began, Doug stood behind a tree as some other Seekers ran past. Wanting to catch his breath, and get up his nerve to make a run for it. Those few seconds he waited slowly ticked by, and Doug scanned the field one more time.

"1, 2, 3," Doug counted slowly and broke into a sprint toward Big Ben.

It felt as if he was in slow motion. Yet he was running as fast as he could.

"He's got the diamond," Bradley Scott yelled, and began to run after him.

"Catch him," Teddy yelled to everyone. Not caring who caught him, just as long as someone did. Doug was hoping it would be a little easier than it was turning out to be.

As Doug ran toward the tree, his worst nightmare happened. Out of his peripheral vision, Doug saw the minesweeper come sprinting out of the woods. Jason Chevrier was at full speed running toward him. All six feet, two hundred pounds of him. Instead of being frozen with fear, Doug shifted into a new gear; deathly afraid Jason would tackle him by mistake. He reached out and touched the tree.

"Incolumitas," he yelled as the fingers on his right hand brushed the tree.

"We won!" Pierce and Skip yelled from their teams' prison.

Doug's fist went into the air, and Jason slowed down in time to only pat Doug on the back. Which happened to hurt just as much as if Doug was punched in the back.

"What is incol..." Jason asked out of breath from his unsuccessful dead sprint.

"I don't know," Doug said with the same worry he had after he made Anna disappear.

"Sorry Manion," Jason apologized for knocking the air out of him. Doug smiled holding in the pain. Both the physical and mental pain of not truly understanding what was going on in his thirteen year-old world.

Parker Gardner blew the horn to signify the end of the game, which meant the end of the championship. Doug, Skip, and Pierce won the championship.

As disappointed as some of the teams were, they clapped anyway.

Pierce saw his Mom drive up in her Honda Element. It wasn't nine- fifteen, but Skip, Doug, and Pierce were happy to be going home, because they were feeling a bit tired. The champions made their way to Pierce's mom's car with the trophy in hand. Doug turned around to the middle of the field and noticed the female referee walking away from the next game.

"That's weird," Doug said kind of to himself and out loud at the same time.

"What's weird?" Skip asked.

"Nothing," Doug thought better of it.

Maybe he was being paranoid, but the female referee was leaving the field before the second game, as if she suddenly got what she needed.

On the drive to drop off Skip, the friends swapped stories about their battle. Not one of them shared their gift, the gift that helped them achieve the win. Saying it out loud would have made it too real for them. Doug and Pierce had no idea that Skip had a gift of her own as well. Pierce found himself staring out the window toward the night sky, anticipating their next adventure.

Chapter 2.3
Toaster Pond

The next morning the summer sun seemed to shine a little bit brighter for the three winners of the Hide-and-Seek Championship. It brightened up the kitchen so much that the three almost had to put on sunglasses. The gold trophy in the middle of the cherry wood table magnified the glow, bringing them to a smile. They deserved it, considering their family woes.

"Where do you want to go today?" Pierce asked Skip and Doug as the three ate breakfast staring at their new golden trophy.

Pierce's Mom left a multitude of food choices for them before she went to work. Skip arrived just in time for the wide array of breakfast treats. Never satisfied with just cereal, Pierce's mom left coffee cake with frosting, Dawn's Delicious Donut Holes and sliced fruit. She always figured fruit would counterbalance all of the fattening treats she provided. Ironically, the three never touched the donuts, only opting for the fruit. They wanted to maintain their health.

The Hide-and-Seek Trophy sat in the middle of the kitchen table. Pierce had a look of pride all morning. There was nothing better to him than winning the coveted Trophy. It wasn't soccer, or another school sport, but most of the athletes from Waterville Junior High were there competing too. Something about Hide-and-Seek was special. It was serious enough to be considered a competition, but still unpolished enough that it would never be a school sport. Pierce loved the recklessness of the whole game. He liked the fact that there were never rude parents cheering on, especially like those at soccer games. The kind that gives sports parents a bad name. Pierce was never fond of bad sportsmanship.

Skip looked pained thinking of a destination for the day. The summer heat was getting to her, but she wanted to celebrate. Her irritation was off-balanced by her pride of winning.

"It's really hot. I don't want to go far," she said with a slight whine. Suddenly, she got a conflicting look on her face as if she couldn't believe the words about to come out of her mouth.

"How about Toaster Pond?" She suggested sounding like she could be swayed into going somewhere else if a better place was thought of in the next few seconds. Perhaps it was bravery talking after last night's win, because Toaster Pond wasn't Skip's favorite place to go.

"Yeah, I could use a swim today," Pierce replied nonchalantly.

Doug nodded his head in agreement, as he busily shoveled down strawberries, grapes, and blueberries; at the same time secretly eyeing Dawn's Delicious Donuts, which were his true favorite.

For some reason Toaster Pond always gave Skip the creeps. It wasn't so much Toaster Pond, as it was the resident who lived across the street.

"Eat fast Manion. By the time we get there your stomach will be settled," Pierce said.

"Thanks Mom," Doug answered sarcastically.

After they cleaned the kitchen table, the three ran out the door. Skip stood up with every ounce of strength she had and grabbed her biking helmet. Pierce noticed her apprehension, which made him laugh a bit because she had suggested the destination. Doug followed them out the door with a donut half-eaten.

"Are you still scared of the Pond?" Pierce asked her as they hopped on their mountain bikes.

"No, it just seems deeper than you guys say it is, that's all."

The boys rolled their eyes at the thought of the shallow pond being very deep.

"We swim in it all the time," Pierce said laughing.

"I know. It just seems…deep," Skip said trying to maintain some ounce of bravery. After all, she had a reputation for being somewhat tough, and was the guard for the Hide-and-Seek team. She didn't want them to know that it wasn't water she was afraid of, but Ethel. Ethel Eisenhut. However, the two boys knew that already.

"Maybe Eisenhut will bring out some lemonade today. Try to be nice to her Skip," Doug suggested jokingly.

"I will be. She just seems too friendly," Skip complained.

"Yeah, I can see how that might be irritating," Doug remarked looking toward Pierce, who was laughing quietly.

Skip rolled her eyes at the friendly teasing. "You know what I mean," she said.

Actually, Doug and Pierce had no idea what Skip meant. They thought Mrs. Eisenhut was a nice woman. A little on the bizarre side, but nice.

Ethel Eisenhut didn't mean to be scary. It just happened. Mostly for the smaller children in town, although she did frighten some of the adults too. Her wealth scared them as well. The Eisenhut Estate was a Waterville favorite. Any out-of-town guests were always treated to a drive by the mansion. It was a way for the residents to show that their small farm town had a lot of class. Although most Waterville residents didn't care what other people thought, because they liked their town the way it was.

Mrs. Eisenhut herself was as spectacular as the estate. She stood about six feet tall, an odd contrast to her husband, who was a few inches shorter. What he lacked in height, he made up in looks. Darkly handsome, with brown eyes and a perfectly trimmed goatee. At least, that was how he looked in pictures. He had been gone for quite some time, and Ethel never really moved on. At least, that's what the non-gifted Waterville residents thought.

Ethel was wafer thin and stood out in a crowd. Much like her estate stood out in Waterville. She had an unusually long nose, and wore a tall tan wicker summer gardening hat. The enormous hat covered her sandy brown hair, making her recognizable to every child in town. They feared that she would turn them into a toad. There would be no doubt, in the minds of the imaginative, that she had a background of being a witch.

The gifted knew she came from a long line of Naylor's, who were a well-known gifted family in Ghent. When she married Henry, it was a powerful union. Gifted always tried to marry gifted.

Doug really liked Ethel because she was a good friend to his late Grandmother Corbin, and she used to come over to his house on occasional Sundays to get her hair cut. Calling Corbin gram his late grandmother, was something Doug was going to have to get used to.

Skip was never there for those Sundays, so she missed out on how nice Mrs. Eisenhut could be. Odd, or artistic was how other people described her.

"You have to get to know her to understand her," was the usual phrase used to describe her, but Ethel didn't care, because she was gifted.

It seemed to be getting hotter by the minute, and Pierce, Doug and Skip were almost to the Pond. With every spin of their pedals, they could feel the sun beating down on them. Sweat was beginning to pour off them as they made their way down Farm Road. The last hill down to the pond provided them with a warm breeze that blew the sweat right off them. Although the breeze was warm, it was cooler than the air, and gave them the moment of relief they were hoping for.

Within a few seconds, they all jumped off their mountain bikes, ready to leap into the pond. The anticipation of cooling off on a hot day made them very cheerful. Toaster Pond looked very inviting, alluring, tempting even, and they were eager to jump in. It was funny, because it actually did look deeper than the registered eight feet that was recorded at Waterville Town Hall.

However, water has a way of doing that. You never have any idea how deep it is by looking at the surface. Much like people. It takes until you jump into a conversation to see if they're deep or shallow.

Out of Skip's peripheral vision she could see Mrs. Eisenhut sitting on her front porch swing with Rufus lying lazily at her large feet. Wearing the tall straw hat and sitting with a long green sundress on, she looked as if she just finished weeding her tremendous garden. No gardeners for hire, Ethel did her own work. It was how she passed the time since Henry passed...over.

"She just got off her broom after an afternoon joy ride," Skip thought to herself.

"Her face does have that wind blown look."

"What's that?" Doug said glancing over at Skip.

"She's outside," Skip warned quietly.

"Hi Wid.... Mrs. Eisenhut," Doug called trying hard not to call her widow.

"Man, you are such a kiss up," Pierce teased, and then he waved with a big smile too. Doug just looked over at him with a sarcastic grin.

"I can't believe you almost called her that," Skip laughed.

"I don't think it's a bad thing. I just would rather call her Mrs. Eisenhut," Doug said.

They hopped off their bikes and pulled off their sneakers and socks.

"You first," Pierce teased Skip.

"Knock it off. I'll go first. I'm not afraid," Skip said.

Her biggest concern was getting past Eisenhut, not the water. Then an eerie feeling came over her that she wasn't expecting. Her tough facade dropped a bit, and she backed away from the water. They all smiled.

"Ok, you go first Doug," Skip said changing her mind.

Doug welcomed the change of heart. He felt it was time to dive in to Toaster Pond.

"STOP...RIGHT...THERE," Mrs. Eisenhut demanded before Doug's big toe broke the surface.

Skip backed up and tried to regain some of her guard strength. It was nowhere to be found. She wanted to be sick or pass out, which ever came first. Doug and Pierce were a little surprised by Mrs. Eisenhut's loud command. Stunned is a better word for it actually. They were sticking up for Eisenhut before they got to Toaster Pond, and here she was yelling at them. Doug second-guessed his friendly wave that he made moments earlier.

Eisenhut began laughing out loud. Doug and Pierce looked confused, one could say scared. Ethel seemed to be the right amount of crazy. Perhaps the heat had gotten to her.

"I'm sorry children, I didn't mean to scare you. I'm just having some fun....Lemonade?" she asked with a smile, and a quick change of conversation.

Her split personality was obviously taking over. Skip's pulse slowed down to a minor heart attack, compared to the major one she was going to have when Ethel first appeared. Pierce and Doug began to laugh uncomfortably; the fear was subsiding. Mrs. Eisenhut spun around for no apparent reason, and in an instant, she had a pitcher of lemonade, and three crystal glasses with ice on a large silver tray. The three teenagers were sure that silver tray was not in her hands when she walked across the road. Not to mention the lemonade and glasses. However, given the occurrences that had taken place since they turned thirteen, Ethel's behavior fit right in. Skip took a seat on a big rock feeling a little stunned, and Pierce and Doug soon joined her. The rocks were hot from the heat of the sun.

"This has got to be sunstroke," Skip said quietly.

Doug, and Pierce barely made out what Skip said, and they slowly shook their head in agreement.

Mrs. Eisenhut knew she startled the children, mostly because she heard Skip's response, and also recognized that they noticed the tray appear in her hands. Ethel gave each one of them a quick glance and decided to come clean.

"Oh that," she said without explaining what she was referring to. She assumed they knew.

"...Oops. I'm sorry. You saw that little trick did you? It's nothing. I have more where that came from. Want to see?" She said quicker with every word.

Her voice was traveling up and down like a roller coaster. It got loud, and then quiet. Ethel was quite proud of herself, and her gift, but she kept trying to tone down her bizarre behavior because she didn't want to scare the children anymore. Although, she knew that they could perform some of the same tricks.

For the first time, in a long time, Pierce, Skip and Doug were all speechless. None of them had any idea what to think, nor what to say.

"Perhaps not," she said quietly looking rather discombobulated.

"The woman has heat stroke," Skip repeated to herself.

"NO, I don't have heatstroke, by the way," Mrs. Eisenhut said eyeing Skip like she read her mind. Skip's heart rate sped up...again.

Mrs. Eisenhut laughed to herself and offered them lemonade once more. Only this time, the glasses were completely full, and they never once noticed her pour the liquid into the glass.

"This is like the other night," Doug mumbled.

"Dear...what's that?" Mrs. Eisenhut asked politely.

"Nothing, Ma'am," Doug lied.

Mrs. Eisenhut's left eye raised and she laughed a little more to herself. She knew it was time for the three kids to cool off in the pond. She feared she did a little too much... crazy... in front of them.

"I'm sorry Dears. I'll let you alone... Please go swimming. I

meant no harm. If you need anything, I'll be right across the road," she said roller coaster like again, raising a glass as if she was going to say cheers and drink a drunken song at the Squealing Pig.

With that she turned on one heel and floated across the road. Pierce recognized the gift of floating, considering he shared the same talent.

"I...think...we...need...to...cool...off." Doug said slowly.

They all stood up and glanced behind them towards Mrs. Eisenhut's direction. She looked up and smiled, then turned her back on them.

"I think Widow Eisenhut IS a witch," Doug said to Skip and Pierce.

"Her husband has been dead for what...ten years. She just figured it out and lost it. She had to. Did you see that," he said with disbelief.

"I think she's drunk," Skip answered back.

"She's not drunk. Drunk people don't float like that across a road,"

Doug answered.

Pierce would have agreed with Doug's comment, but knew that the shock of the day was only going to get worse for his two best friends.

The sun was shining brighter and hotter than it had in days. The three friends took off their sneakers and left them on the beach. Pierce and Doug left their shirts there as well.

"You're going first," Skip said to Doug.

Pierce agreed with Skip. Each one let their toes touch the water. All three felt a wonderful tingling sensation cover their bodies as their big toes flirted with the water, and they felt instantly comfortable. Not cool, no longer hot, just the perfect temperature. The strange thing about it was, that the water didn't feel wet, like water should feel. It felt like they were putting their feet into a tub of warm air. The kind of air that Doug felt on his cheek two nights ago before he went to sleep. It gave them a feeling of absolute calmness.

Ethel Eisenhut's strange behavior was now a thing of the past, and they were becoming increasingly focused on the future. Almost entranced by the feeling of the water.

Skip glanced over at Pierce who was giggling uncontrollably at the feeling of the magical water on his toes. Doug wasn't sure what they were walking into, but he knew he wanted to keep taking steps.

Ethel Eisenhut was watching the three teenagers from her living room window. She was smiling as they took their first steps into the mysterious Toaster Pond. Ethel watched, as their ankles were completely submerged. Mrs. Eisenhut knew all of the friends very well, and she knew they were most deserving of all of the newly turned teenagers in Waterville. She worked diligently at choosing the right teenagers for the important adventure they were about to begin. She watched as the water rose around their knees.

"Bingo," she said to Rufus. "I've got them."

Rufus made his usual dog noise, and put his head back down on the porch floor determined not to let the commotion across the street ruin his chance at an afternoon nap.

"You first...," Skip dared Doug.

"I was first getting in here," Doug said reminding Skip.

Without any more fear, Doug took another step into the pond and the water reached his waist.

As Doug was taking each step into Toaster Pond, he knew that the events from two nights ago must be tied into the events they were experiencing now. It was all too strange not to be connected. He was waist deep in the water. As was Pierce. Skip was a little more ambivalent about going under.

Doug began thinking about the past few days. First, a thunderstorm that came out of nowhere. Second, a soft voice in the hallway, calling his name. Third, an old woman who disappeared because he wanted her too. And then finding out later that she was home, completely stunned by the fact that she passed out and appeared in her own home without remembering how she got there. Her friends thought she was nuts. Doug knew better. Finally, a complete stranger at the game of Hide-and-Seek who seemed to be watching them.

At this point he was mesmerized by the tingling sensation of the water. It surrounded him and completely encompassed his thoughts. Toaster Pond felt enchanting to all three teenagers.

Doug turned around to tell Pierce and Skip to take another step, and when he did, Mrs. Eisenhut was in the window, smiling, mouthing the words,

"Have fun," and stepped away out of sight.

Doug wasn't nervous at all. He felt like he was being protected and that he was safe. Waterville always felt magical, and now he was experiencing everything it had to offer.

"Come on. Let's go in headfirst," he suggested to the others as the water surrounded his chest.

"Sounds good to me," Skip agreed, feeling secure.

The feeling of the water was intriguing her as it covered her waist.

"Are we under some spell," Doug thought to himself. Nothing about the moment bothered him and he was ready to let go and see where the water took him.

He didn't want to mention it out loud to his two friends because they might think he was crazy. However, Pierce knew exactly what they were walking into, because his father explained it all to him when he turned thirteen; just before Dr. Butterworth "disappeared" and left for Sanger Castle.

The water rose up around them, like a favorite blanket on a cold night. And even though it was the middle of a hot summer, the warm blanket feeling of Toaster Pond felt soothing. Mrs. Eisenhut was back at the window of her house peeking out. She couldn't help herself from being nosey.

Skip's gift began to take over and at first was nervous about her friends hearing it. Remembering the fateful day when she turned thirteen and received a gift in the mail. No return address. Thinking it was an item her Dad won on E-Bay, she bent over to pick it up and saw her name.

Skip Corbin

18 Pinewood Road

Waterville

Opening the mysterious package, there was a book of spells. Skip immediately opened and began reading the book. After a few hours of putting the book under her pillow, trying to forget about it, she gained the strength to give a spell a try. As she read the book, her dog Muffin pushed open the door and Skip had an idea. She tried one on Muffin, and was surprised to see the dog go from a black poodle to an apricot one.

A bookmark appeared in the Book of Spells that day. The bookmark simply said, "Use this spell wisely." Wading in Toaster Pond, Skip knew this was the time to use that spell.

"Walk in deeper

Until your knees are wet.

You're on an adventure

You won't forget.
The water flows
Around your chest,
This adventure,
Will be your best.
The water climbs
Above your head.
Your path will go,
Where you have said."

Mrs. Eisenhut kept looking out the window and she saw the kids disappearing. Hoping for the best, she crossed her fingers and silently wished them good luck.

Doug and Pierce looked over at Skip, and they all realized at the same time that each friend was bringing a different gift to Toaster Pond. It was almost as if destiny caused them to become friends.

All three were completely relaxed, sinking down toward the bottom. The bottom that once housed an old toaster, thrown in by an old woman angry that her husband bought her a toaster for their fiftieth anniversary.

It was odd. The three never had been able to hold their breath this long before. All three were perfectly fine, sinking deeper under the water. It never occurred to them, possibly because of the shock of the whole event, that they were sinking much further than the eight foot depth that was on record at Waterville Town Hall. Skip was usually chastised for her argument of it being deeper than it looked. She didn't think now was a time for "I told you so's."

Pierce looked over at Skip and they smiled to each other through the clear blue water. The pond had not seemed that clear to the three when they walked or drove by it, but it was crystal clear when they sunk down into it. After looking at each other far underneath the surface of the pond, all three closed their eyes and began to rise up toward the surface again. Feeling a little disappointed at the anticlimactic ending to their adventure, they swam toward the top of Toaster Pond.

Skip's red hair popped up out of the water first, then the dark black hair of Pierce Butterworth came out, finally the sandy brown crew cut of Doug Manion broke the surface.

Pierce and Skip looked around at new scenery, mouths hanging open. It was exactly like Pierce had imagined it in his dreams after the stories his father told him. They couldn't believe their eyes. They were careful not to swallow water even though their mouths were hanging wide open. The three teenagers were still floating in Toaster Pond, but Toaster Pond seemed to be located somewhere other than Waterville.

"Welcome to Sangerfield," Pierce said with a laugh, spitting out water.

"Sangerfield?" Doug said with confusion.

Skip floated in the water, staring around at the trees and noticed their clothes on the beach.

"What haven't you told us," Skip asked Pierce inquisitively, with a little flare of anger.

"I think we "all" have some explaining to do," Pierce said.

The weather was as beautiful as when they left Waterville, but it was not nearly as hot. They swam toward the beach and found three towels and their shirts and sneakers exactly where they left them. It was as if they were still swimming in Waterville, not this mysterious place called Sangerfield. They dried off and put on their socks and sneakers. All three stared at their surroundings.

It took a few minutes for the three friends to speak. Doug knew the inevitable had to happen.

"While we're here, why not explore?" Doug suggested.

"Which way do you want to go?" Skip asked.

"Not that way," Pierce said pointing toward the woods as if he knew why, but didn't want to say.

There was something eerie about the massive number of dark trees in rows, like they were standing guard for someone... or something.

"Then I guess we can walk that way," Doug suggested pointing toward a path that looked a little sunnier.

Skip thought she saw a figure in the woods before she turned to look at the path. She dried her eyes to get a better look, but no one was there.

"Skip, did you hear me?" Doug asked shortly, wondering why Skip was preoccupied.

"No," she said feeling a bit unfocused.

"I said we can walk that way," Doug said pointing toward the trail a second time.

Skip agreed, and they made their way through the path. Along the way they each began to explain the strange occurrences that had taken place since turning thirteen.

Doug explained how he made the woman disappear.

"She kept pinching my cheeks and I wanted her to get away from me," he explained.

"And she just disappeared?" Skip asked in awe.

"Poof, she was gone," Doug said in return.

He explained how he had disappeared during the Hide-and-Seek Championship when he used the necklace his father gave him for his birthday.

"And they walked right past you," Skip asked.

"Teddy Hemmings almost stepped on my foot," Doug explained.

Skip told them about the Book of Spells and Muffin's new apricot fur.

"It was my name and no return address," she said.

"Did you recognize the handwriting?" Doug asked.

"Yeah, but it wouldn't make sense," Skip said.

"Try me," Doug asked.

"It looked like Corbin Gram's," Skip said quietly. "I think she sent it right before she died."

Doug kept walking but felt shocked. Pierce didn't offer as much information as he could have. The other surprises were worth waiting for.

For once, Pierce felt like the one who was smart, and felt powerful knowing secret information.

While they were walking over the plush green grass and rolling hills, Pierce explained the fact that he could float like Mrs.

Eisenhut. Skip and Doug noticed that Pierce appeared to be confident walking around in their new surroundings. Almost as if he had been there before, or, he was completely confident that they were going in the right direction. Pierce decided to let them in on a secret that they would eventually find out anyway. He told them that his father, Dr. Butterworth did disappear but he and his mom knew his whereabouts. Pierce didn't offer up any immediate details.

The separation between the path and trees looked like it had an imaginary barrier, the trees were aligned perfectly, and not one of them stood out of place. A tree branch broke in the forest beside them, and all three looked over instantly. Nothing, or no one was there, but whatever broke it had to be big, because the woods were deep and the crack was loud. Skip felt that she saw something earlier, but no matter how much she looked, there wasn't anything in sight. The noise didn't help the three anxious travelers. They could feel themselves become chilled because of the noise, and it cemented the decision not to go through the woods.

They didn't know that they were following the same path Vernon and Effie Eisenhut, Horatio and Virginia Sanger, and Mustafa and Lucinda Zwevil had walked nearly one hundred years earlier.

PART II SANGER CASTLE

Chapter 3.0 Sangerfield

S kip, Doug and Pierce began walking up a rather steep hill covered with tall green grass, and each swore they heard someone giggle from a few feet away. They stopped suddenly and looked around. The deep green grass was flowing with the soft wind that blew across the Sangerfield hills.

"Hheeeheeeheee," came a small giggle again, but when they looked, no one was there.

Pierce pointed toward some grass in close proximity to them, and it was moving as if someone was running through it, but they couldn't see anyone. They all looked at each other in disbelief, each with a little bit of fear. They were not sure if it was an animal that caused the rustling or the wind.

They climbed to the top of the grassy hill and couldn't believe what they saw in the distance. Water was flowing over a waterfall. The sound the water made when it crashed against the rocks and large pool below was deafening. Never in their lives had two of the three friends ever seen something so enormous. Small streams took off in every direction from the large pool that held the rushing water. It looked like nature made its own irrigation system.

"Oriskany Falls," Pierce said simply, and began walking ahead of his friends.

"What's that?" Doug asked following closely behind him.

"It's Oriskany Falls. We're almost there," Pierce answered.

"Almost where?" Doug asked.

Pierce kept walking as if he knew they were on a time schedule.

"Pierce. Stop!" Skip yelled realizing that he was being coy.

Pierce stopped in his tracks. Skip was a little more intimidating than Doug at the moment. He turned around and faced his two best friends, knowing it was time to share some of the truth.

"What is going on?" Skip asked.

Pierce took a deep breath as if to give himself enough time to find a believable and worthwhile answer.

"We are at Oriskany Falls. It's been here for hundreds of years. It's a sacred place in Sangerfield. We need to keep walking past it, and then you'll see why we're here," he said sounding as if he had been there many times. "We're expected for a Hide-and-Seek tournament at Sanger Castle. The place is amazing. I promise you that it will be worth the pain of getting there. I've never been there but I've seen pictures," Pierce said to make his friends believe he didn't have an unfair advantage.

With that being said, Pierce turned around and began walking forward, eyes closed, praying that his friends would follow in his footsteps. Skip and Doug were shocked, and a little too angry to ask any more questions. They put their heads down and followed Pierce. He had never steered them the wrong way before, and they were hoping he wasn't turning over a new leaf. However, the silence between the three friends was deafening.

After they walked past Oriskany Falls, they jumped over one of the streams that was in their way and began to climb up a steep path. They finished hiking up a small wooded mountain. At the crest of the mountain they stood in silence. Larger than any estate in Waterville, stood what obviously had to be Sanger Castle.

"Those woods go pretty far," Doug said noticing the trees that were aligned on the side of the path that led to Sanger Castle.

"The forest is huge. I wouldn't want to get lost in there," Pierce said.

"Hopefully we won't have to go in the forest," Skip piped in.

Pierce was actually hoping the opposite.

All three friends stood staring at the forest to the left of the castle, which was connected to the trail that they had been walking on for an hour. Looking to the right, they saw the rolling green hills that led through Sangerfield. They couldn't help noticing that the whole area ahead of them looked like something out of a painting.

Smack in the middle of the forest and the rolling hills, stood Sanger Castle. It was a large medieval castle made out of dark brick, stood surrounded by a 15-foot flag stone wall, and was breathtakingly beautiful. It reminded Doug of the photos of the castles his Uncle Murph showed him from Europe.

"That place is huge," Doug said in awe.

Skip was in awe. "Huge? I've never seen anything so big in my life."

"How many rooms do you think are in there?" Doug asked looking at Pierce, realizing he may know that information.

"I don't know. Maybe a thousand," Pierce said guessing, not really sure if it was an exaggeration.

"That's a lot of rooms," Skip and Doug said together.

Although they had never seen the castle before, it seemed somewhat familiar to them. A large bell began ringing, and the sound echoed through Sangerfield. The grass in the field seemed to be waving in different directions, but the grass was too high to see if it was waving because of the wind, or because of something or someone else.

"I have never seen anything so huge in my life," Skip said for the second time, staring at the castle.

Her mood was changing from anxious to anticipation of what was to come. Although she had no idea what that was, she found herself ready for an adventure.

The three began their slow descent down the embankment toward the castle. As much information as Pierce seemed to have, he still didn't know what was going to happen when they reached the castle.

"Why didn't you tell us?" Doug asked his best friend breaking the uncomfortable silence.

"I was told not to," Pierce answered.

"But we're your best friends," Skip piped in with a little anger in her voice.

"Yeah, but it's my father who asked me not to say anything," Pierce said turning around to look at both of them.

Doug knew he didn't need to push it any further. Friends are important, but all three had strong bonds with their parents. Skip stopped asking questions as well, and just followed as Pierce led them down a path toward the castle. Their tired feet kicked up rocks and dirt to the final sounds of the bell tolling.

Walking through the field next to the wall surrounding the castle, they all knew they were about to enter someplace amazing. Pierce felt confident, and sort of at home. Doug and Skip had a mixture of feelings, but trusted Pierce wholeheartedly. As they continued walking, three kids around their age were walking toward them. The one boy and two girls had what only could be described as team t-shirts on, with shorts and sneakers. Their shirts were red with black polka dots.

"Hello," the three said staring strangely at Doug, Skip and Pierce. They said hello back and kept walking. Too stunned to stop for a conversation, the three Waterville teenagers crossed the entrance of the castle and made their way toward the enormous double doors that stood in the front.

Doug's eyes focused on the massive door knockers that hung on each one of the double doors. Skip's were on the three teenagers walking away. The golden knockers were triangular shaped. He had seen the same symbol when reading science fantasy books, and remembered the symbol meant something sacred.

"What are you looking at?" Skip asked, noticing Doug's stare when she turned back around.

"That symbol on the door $\triangle$ it means something. I've read it somewhere before," he began explaining.

"Well?" Skip asked feeling impatient for her cousin's answer.

"It means power or three or safety or something," Doug said staring at the odd symbol feeling a bit confused. His answer didn't help Skip at all.

"Who goes there?" Boomed a mysterious voice from above.

The three stopped in their tracks and looked up nervously. A guard tower appeared at the top of the stone wall.

"I didn't even see that one coming," Skip said quietly.

The voice from above turned from serious to laughter. All three stared up at the guard tower but the sun blinded them enough that they could not focus on the person yelling.

"We're..." Skip began to stutter trying to think of something to say.

Introducing themselves was the best plan of action that Skip could come up with, and Doug and Pierce weren't very helpful at the moment. Pierce had seen pictures of the castle but had never been there. As much information as he had, a feeling of nervousness came over him as the booming voice continued.

"I know who you are," the guard announced from behind them.

Skip, Doug, and Pierce turned around to get a look at the face behind the voice. He stood over six feet tall, had dark brown hair, he looked to be an older man of about forty. Wearing a dark black cloak, which accented his dark hair, his piercing green eyes made Skip feel a little distracted.

"You must be Skip, Doug and Pierce," he said looking at all three, knowing exactly who was who.

"And by the way... the symbol..." he began pointing toward the doors ahead of them,

"Does mean three, which is a sacred number. It also means power and safety. Symbols are my expertise," the unfamiliar man said with pride.

Doug was feeling very pleased with himself. Skip rolled her eyes at her cousins feeling of smugness for knowing the answer.

"How... do... you...know...our...names?" Doug asked slowly realizing that the man knew who they were.

"I've, well, we've been expecting you. No one comes here without our knowing," he said smiling.

"I'm sorry about the "who goes there stuff." I like to do that for shock value." He smiled a bit more, and shook his head remembering his manners.

"How rude of me. My name is Baron Jody D. Doha. Welcome to Sanger Castle," he announced turning toward the castle with his arms open wide.

"That's a name to try to remember," Doug thought to himself.

"What do you do here?" Skip asked bravely.

Baron Doha laughed a bit, and said, "Do? What one does is complicated. I welcome newcomers to our castle, I study ancient symbols, and I experiment with...I'll explain more later."

Sounding as if he impressed himself, he realized that the teenagers were a bit culture shocked. Thinking quickly, he did what any self-respecting adult would do. He changed the subject.

"Come with me, please. You must be FAMISHED from your trip," he said loudly with a gentle grin.

Skip walked right behind him, not needing too much prodding to follow Doha. Pierce and Doug were giggling behind her because of the innocent trance that the Baron had over Skip so quickly. Skip, however, was becoming confident about her surroundings and wanted to be a bit more inquisitive. After all, the symbol on the door meant safety. Obviously other kids her age were around as well, so the castle allowed teenagers in. She just didn't understand why they were there.

"Pierce told us we're here for the Hide-and-Seek competition," Doug began as they were walking.

"Yes," The Baron answered looking at Pierce with a smile.

"Why is there a competition here," Doug asked.

"We'll explain later," Pierce said knowing that his friends were going to be a little angry with him.

Doug and Skip remained quiet; trying to figure out why Pierce had not been forthcoming with all of information he seemed to have.

As they walked in the door of the castle, they could not believe their eyes. The corridor that led the residents through the castle was the size of a house. The great hallway was filled with pictures of children that spanned hundreds of years. All of the pictures were in black and white, with silver triangular frames, except for one that was gold. Passing quickly by the gold framed picture, the kids in the photo looked familiar to Doug but he wasn't sure why.

Pierce was staring in awe at the sheer size of the hallway and the ceiling that was twenty feet above their heads. The pictures his dad hand shown him of the castle did not do it justice. It was much more amazing in person.

All three followed the Baron as he walked through the corridor into the great hallway. The sound of a musical instrument came from somewhere in the castle.

"What's that sound?" Pierce asked stopping to listen to the odd noise.

"It's a lute," Baron Doha explained.

"What's a lute?" Skip asked.

"It's an old medieval instrument that was used hundreds of years ago. We have a few prof...people that play it here," Doha said. "Slap, slap," The sound of his black leather shoes slapped against the hard ceramic floor.

There wasn't much of a conversation taking place because the three teenagers were staring around the castle taking it all in.

All four began walking faster, as if they were on an important mission. Baron Doha and Pierce understood how important the mission was, but Doug and Skip had no clue. They made their way to a large entrance going into what could only be described as the biggest library they had ever seen.

The three teenagers weren't sure how many books had ever been written, but they were sure that this library housed them all. Waterville Junior High School could have fit in the castle library alone. Fireplaces were on four sides of the room, and they were burning, even though it was summer. The room wasn't really hot, or cold. The temperature seemed to be a perfect seventy-two degrees.

As the three took in the sight of the library, they noticed signs explaining the categories of books. Skip and Doug were excited to see the enormous Science section, because that was their favorite subject. It had to be; their favorite grandmother taught it for thirty years. The section on symbols caught their eye because of the discussion they had moments before.

"What is going on?" Doug whispered to Pierce as he saw a section on Dark Magic.

Pierce pointed over to the young man coming toward them.

The young man seemed to be walking in slow motion. Either that or Doug and Skip were still in shock.

They could not believe who was standing in front of them. The lights flickered, and then went out. It was completely dark in the gargantuan library, except for the light from the fireplaces. As if Skip and Doug were not anxious enough, the young man standing in front of them was someone they knew quite well from Waterville.

"I have got to be dreaming," Doug said out loud.

"Then if you are, we're dreaming the same dream. I mean everyone but Pierce," Skip answered back with a bit of sarcasm in her voice.

Pierce knew he would have to fully explain everything. The lights came back on in the library. Skip and Doug stood frozen in the middle of the room. Pierce just smiled and felt like everything was coming full circle.

"Parker Gardner. What are you doing here?" Doug asked in disbelief.

Parker looked over at the Baron, who in return looked at Parker and nodded.

"I came to meet up with the three of you," he began.

"We knew you were coming," he continued.

"Why does everyone say that?" Doug asked.

"When gifted children enter the pond, certain important people in Sanger Castle know they're coming," Parker explained.

"How do they know?" Doug asked waiting for a magical answer.

"We have look-outs," Parker said smiling.

"Are you one of them?" Doug asked not totally sure he wanted the answer.

"Look-out...sort of, gifted-yes, but not like the professors and barons," Parker clarified.

"What do you do here?" Skip asked, hoping she would get a better answer than the vague one Doha gave her.

"I sort of run the sports program here," he answered with a smile.

Baron Doha smiled a bit as well.

"Huh?" Skip said confused.

"What is this place? Why haven't we ever heard of it before?" Doug asked.

"I'll explain it all soon," Parker answered understanding the magnitude of his answer.

All of the secrecy was necessary, none of the adults had time to give Skip and Doug the full answer they deserved and much needed.

Doug and Skip however, couldn't help but notice that Pierce was smiling as if he was extremely happy about the current events. Feeling totally confident that when his friends met everyone involved, they would forgive him for holding back.

"How about some lunch?" the Baron suggested in a loud voice that echoed in the empty library.

"Shhh," the lone librarian said from behind her desk.

"I'm very sorry Ms. Herr," the Baron apologized to the impatient woman.

Coming from around her desk, she nodded and smiled at him. Turning toward the three teenagers, Ms. Herr gave them a warm smile as well and said welcome. Then she floated away. Skip and Doug stared at her with amazement. Then they turned toward Pierce who was grinning widely.

"Ms. Herr is the best librarian you will ever meet," the Baron said seriously as he checked his watch.

"Why don't you take them to the dining hall, and then on a tour of the unrestricted places in the castle?" he continued.

Parker nodded his head in agreement, and pointed toward the exit from the library.

"Lunch should be starting in a few minutes. Shall we?" and the four teenagers began walking slowly toward the great hallway.

Baron Doha walked quietly the opposite way past Ms. Herr.

As the four teenagers made their way down the hallway, the lights flickered again.

"Why are the lights doing that?" Doug asked.

"It's... nothing. I'll explain later," Parker said abruptly.

"If it's nothing, why explain it later?" Doug thought to himself.

The hallway looked like a typical hallway from their school. Only ten times the size. The walls that didn't have triangular pictures hanging on them, had hundreds of trophy cases against them instead. Doug couldn't help but notice that one of the pictures had a black cloth hanging over it. He had his choice of pictures to look at, but the fact that a black cloth covered one made him want to see it all the more. He pointed to it and Skip looked.

"What's wrong with this picture?" Skip asked pointing to the covered one. Parker stopped, and seemed a bit taken aback.

"We don't talk about that one," Parker said solemnly.

"If you can't look at it, and can't see it, why not take it down then?" asked Skip.

"We can't take down the pictures of those who came before us, even if we disagree with their choices," Parker explained vaguely.

"What choices?" Doug asked.

Parker knew he said too much, and realized how much he was avoiding every question Doug and Skip asked.

"Another time. We have enough to worry about," he said redirecting them toward their destination.

About fifty yards ahead of them, kids around their age walked into what looked to be a room, although they hadn't quite reached it. There seemed to be a lot of excitement, and it must have been infectious because Pierce, Skip, and Doug were beginning to feel excited as well. As they got closer, they realized it was a huge cafeteria with adjoining dining hall. Everything in the castle was on a grand scale, and the cafeteria and dining hall were no exceptions. The room was massive with chandeliers hanging from many spots on the ceiling.

The young people they saw walking around were wearing shorts, and had T-shirts on that seemed to belong to a variety of teams. Some of the shirts were maroon, blue, yellow, and various other colors. Not just red, like the kids from outside.

Doug, Skip, and Pierce were looking around in awe, and it

multiplied as they walked into the cafeteria from the dining hall.

"This is the refectory," Parker announced to them as they walked in the doorway. "What's a refectory?" Skip asked.

"It's a fancy word for cafeteria," Parker answered.

"Where did all of these kids come from?" Skip wondered aloud.

"Well, they're not from Waterville, if that's what your're asking," he answered.

"I didn't think they were. I've never seen any of them before," she answered back.

Actually, Skip, Doug, and Pierce had never seen so many kids in one place before. The size of the refectory alone was bigger than their whole school. Add on the dining hall, and the place was overwhelming.

As Doug, Skip, Pierce and Parker walked in, some of the kids stopped eating and looked over at them. A few of the kids said hello, and others seemed to be whispering to each other. However, there were many children who were too busy eating to be bothered looking at the three newcomers entering the room.

Just as they were getting used to the magnitude of the situation, the lights flickered again. Most of the kids, who were eating, stopped. Some stared at the lights above, and others stared toward the general direction of Parker. Pierce and Skip didn't notice because they were too awed by the situation, but Doug recognized the fact that Parker had an obvious importance compared to every person eating in the dining hall.

Doug, Skip, Pierce, and Parker grabbed trays, and what lay ahead of them was the biggest buffet that three of the four had ever seen in their lives. Pizza, shrimp, egg rolls, food from every nation around the globe was lying in front of them, waiting for someone to pick it up to be devoured. Doug wondered how many chefs it took to prepare this much food.

"Are these the choices everyday?" Skip asked.

She was obviously thinking the same thing Doug was.

"We usually don't have this much, but this weekend is special," Parker answered.

"Dinner is usually prepared for us, and breakfast happens at different times for different dormitories." Parker stopped suddenly realizing that he said too much.

"Dormitories… do all of these kids sleep here?" Skip asked.

"They come and go only during the summer. Sort of like summer camp for the Gifted. But in a few months they may stay for a longer period of time. That mostly depends on how tomorrow goes." Parker answered.

Before Doug or Skip could get a question out, Parker stopped them.

"Ah, ah, ah, in due time. I promise. Most of them are here for the competition. Some are family members of the barons. I'll explain when we sit down," he said. "We'll go over there and eat our lunch," Parker suggested pointing to an empty table.

The four teenagers grabbed their food filled trays and walked to an open cherry wood table. It was solid and seemed very heavy. Not like the cafeteria tables they were used to from Waterville Junior High.

Like a deer in headlights, Doug couldn't quite gain the composure to stop himself from gawking at the other kids and the grown-ups who were sitting at the head table.

The three newbies became well aware that they were somewhere special, and they also understood that they stood out from everyone for some reason. Doug and Skip were eager to find out why. Pierce knew the reason, and wanted to wait until the surprise guests arrived to explain everything.

"I'll explain as much as I can. You guys were a little later than we expected," Parker explained.

Skip and Doug looked at each other. Being late meant they were expected to arrive. However they had no idea traveling was a part of the plan when they stepped foot in Toaster Pond. Pierce, however, must have known the whole time.

"I understand that you have no idea what's going on and I apologize for that, but we needed you here. Lord Eisenhut will explain the competition phase of the experience. I'll explain the rest after lunch is finished," Parker confided, knowing that Doug and Skip were still in shock and only understood about half of what he told them.

Pierce was actually beginning to feel better about the situation. Ironically, it was when his two best friends were beginning to feel worse about it.

"Lord Eisenhut?" Doug asked astounded.

"Yes, Eisenhut," Parker answered as if he knew what the three were thinking.

"Eisenhut isn't a common name," Skip said bluntly.

"No, it's not," Parker answered matter-of-factly.

"Which one is Lord Eisenhut?" Doug asked.

Parker pointed toward an older looking man of about fifty or sixty, who was wearing a robe like that of Baron Doha, only Doha's was black, and Eisenhut's was maroon. He had a salt and pepper goatee and a Julius Caesar styled haircut. He looked very distinguished, as if he was the most important person in the castle, which he was.

"That is Lord Eisenhut," Parker enlightened.

"How could that be Widow Eisenhut's husband?" Doug asked. "He doesn't look dead," he said politely.

Skip slowly shook her head in agreement. Parker laughed a bit.

"We have a lot to explain to you," Pierce chimed in.

"You mean you're finally going to say something?" Skip said sounding annoyed.

"Please don't be angry with Pierce. He was sworn to secrecy," Parker said defending Pierce.

"By whom?" Doug asked using proper English.

"By Eisenhut and my dad," Pierce began.

"Listen guys. I know you're a little upset with me but I had a good reason," Pierce confided.

"Give me one," Doug asked.

Unfortunately, Pierce couldn't come up with one. Or rather, he didn't want to, because it would ruin the surprise.

Although they were a bit nervous, they were also hungry. Skip and Doug were devouring their food.

"Take it easy guys. No one's going to take it away from you," Pierce said trying to break the tension. Doug and Skip looked a little embarrassed and began to eat a little slower.

The dining hall was bustling with excitement and with it came noise. The kids sitting around the tables were all whispering and talking with one another. Much to Doug and Skip's astonishment, no one ever stood up to throw their food out or empty their trays. And yet, there were no trays to be found in front of most of the hundreds of kids sitting around the numerous tables in the dining hall.

As soon as Doug and Skip finished eating, they were about to stand up to throw their things away, and the trays simply disappeared into the hard cherry wood table in front of them. They looked at each other in amazement, and Parker and Pierce began to giggle at the obviously confused looks on their faces.

"I'll give you two reasons why I didn't say anything," Pierce began, feeling ready to let loose.

Unfortunately, he was interrupted by a more important figure in Sanger Castle Royalty. "May I have your attention please," a voice boomed over the crowd. Doug and Skip were staring expectantly at Pierce waiting to hear reasons he kept everything so quiet, but Eisenhut was too amazing to be ignored.

With almost one hundred tables placed in the dining hall, the simple sound of one voice made everyone stop talking. Standing at the head table, which was on a stage in front of them, stood Lord Eisenhut.

"Thank you. And welcome to Sanger Castle," he said with a smile.

"It's nice to see some of you back, and some new faces as well," he announced looking over at Skip, Doug and Pierce.

Doug couldn't help but notice that almost everyone was staring at his table too. He felt like an outcast, which could not have been further from the truth.

"After you leave the dining hall, you will get your room assignments if you haven't already. The competition will begin tomorrow morning at 8:00 a.m. Rules will be posted outside your dormitories on the announcement boards. Please make sure you have a spot saved for your confinement by nightfall. I don't want anyone entering the fields after dark," Lord

Eisenhut warned as his voice lowered with every word spoken. And with that, he turned, walked off the stage and out the door. "This is going to be so cool," Doug thought to himself. Unfortunately, Doug had no idea it was going to be more dangerous than cool.

Chapter 3.1
Don't You Get It?

"I 'll walk the three of you to get your assignments. I'll explain everything along the way," Parker assured Skip and Doug as they walked out of the dining hall. "I'll tell you my part too," Pierce said trying to get back on the good side of his friends.

Doug thought it better be a long walk, because there seemed to be a lot that needed to be explained, and apparently it all needed to be heard before dark.

"I know you've been patient, and I thank you for that, but there is a reason for all of the secrecy," Parker confided. It was beginning to sound like the same speech over and over again to Doug and Skip. Secrecy was a word used a lot in conversations at Sanger Castle.

Parker wasn't sure where to begin. Most of the gifted newcomers didn't have scattered information like Skip and Doug. However, most of the newcomers weren't as gifted as the three who were walking with him.

"Mrs. Eisenhut is married to Lord Eisenhut, so she's actually considered a Lady here. He's not really dead, obviously. He's just passed on to another, some might say better place, which happens to be Sangerfield," Parker began.

Doug couldn't help but catch the phrase, "better place," because his father had used it a few days earlier.

"Sangerfield is a place you can't get to by car, but it's a short trip when you go through Toaster Pond. It exists, it's just that non-gifted people will never find it," Pierce added.

Doug and Skip looked over. "How do you know so much about it?" they asked at the same time.

"My father is here," Pierce said. Doug and Skip stopped in their tracks.

"What do you mean your father is here," Doug asked.

His freckled face was beginning to get red.

"He works here at the castle. He left the college to do research here with Eisenhut," Pierce explained bluntly.

"My father didn't want me to say anything to you until you both started to show signs of progressing."

"What kind of research," Doug asked.

"Magical herbs, portals, and good versus evil," Pierce answered.

"Just your everyday research," he said smiling.

Doug and Skip both could not help but notice how intelligent Pierce sounded. As if the castle suddenly made him smarter.

"What did you mean by progressing?" Skip asked, ignoring for the moment, the fact that Pierce mentioned magical herbs and portals.

"Don't you guys get it?" Pierce said stopping in the middle of the main corridor looking at his two best friends.

"You both have noticed that you can do things. You told me about them on the path," Pierce said feeling a bit excited. All the weeks of holding it in were about to explode. The mixed feelings he had a few weeks earlier had disappeared, and he found himself excited about something. That something was being gifted.

"Your wearing a necklace that helps you disappear," Pierce began. "But it's not just the necklace. It's the necklace and your abilities."

"And you," he began by looking at Skip.

"What about me?" Skip said defensively.

"You use a spell you read in a Book of Spells, that you mysteriously got as a gift. And you suddenly can make you and two of your best friends go from one portal to another," Parker chimed in.

Skip looked over at Pierce, wondering how Parker could

possibly know the information, when she just shared it with Doug and Pierce on the way to the castle.

"We're meant to be here," Pierce said seriously.

"We're gifted." Doug and Skip stared at their friend for a moment. It was sinking in that they might never be the same again.

"You both explained everything that has been happening," Pierce continued.

"You made that old woman disappear. Your mind is stronger than a non-gifted person. You can make objects disappear. And not just any objects. Non-gifted people. It's not that you hurt them; they just appear back where they belong. And they can't really tell the difference because they talk themselves out of realizing the truth."

"And Skip. You have a gift for spells and herbs, it just isn't mastered yet." Pierce said.

"What about you?" Doug asked the inevitable question.

"I'm not sure what my gift is yet. I mean I can do beginner stuff like most other gifted people. But, I like studying about the gift more than I can do it," Pierce continued.

"You study," Doug asked sarcastically, never remembering Pierce to be much of a scholar. After all, he barely made it out of seventh grade.

"I know. Can you believe it?" Pierce said. "But this is different. It's just...it's so cool! Our...we, I have been reading about it so much because I just totally believe in this. And you will too," he said matter-of-factly.

Doug and Skip were already believers, it was just taking them a while to take all of the information in, and rationalize it. It wasn't typical for every thirteen year old to wake up and figure out they have a gift.

As if the shock from the conversation wasn't enough, the lights flickered again. Parker began walking and motioned for the three teenagers to follow.

"You've experienced the light flickering twice since you've been here," Parker began after taking many steps. "The castle runs on energy, but not the type of energy we have back at home in Waterville. It's energy taken from special gems. Unfortunately, we're running out of energy," Parker explained.

"So get more gems," Skip suggested quickly, as if no one else had thought of that.

"It's not that easy," Parker began. "We can only get gems from inside Shadow Forest," he said. "Unfortunately, the forest is protected by Ludicrous Zwevil. She would like nothing better than to have the castle run out of energy so she can take it over. The one with the gem provides the energy and possesses the real power."

"No gem, no protection," Pierce said.

"Why hasn't she tried to take over the castle?" Doug asked.

"Because she's afraid of Eisenhut." Parker said.

"Why can't Lord Eisenhut go in and get them if he is so powerful?" Skip said.

"He's not capable of going into the forest," Parker answered.

"No adult above the age of seventeen can go into the forest. Spells are a wonderful thing, but unfortunately, spells can do as much harm as good. It depends on who has the spell," he continued. "Ludicrous Zwevil put a spell on Shadow Forest, and no one can find a counter-spell. They've tried for many, many years," Parker said knowing full well that would initiate a response.

"Many, many years," Doug and Skip said in unison.

"How long has this place been here?" Skip asked.

"This land has been here forever. Lord Eisenhut is a Lord in a long line of Eisenhut's who've practiced magic. Just as Ludicrous Zwevil had many ancestors who practiced magic. She's the second Zwevil who wanted to practice dark magic. Her father wanted to rule the land, but the Eisenhuts won and have reigned ever since," Parker said proudly.

"Why is it called Sanger Castle?" Skip asked inquisitively.

"Lord Sanger was killed in a duel of wands with Mustafa Zwevil,"
Parker explained.

"Wands?" Doug asked disbelievingly.

"Yes, magical wands," Parker answered.

"What is a magical wand?" Doug asked a second time.

"It's an ancient weapon used by gifted people. They either use wands or staves, which is a staff. We find those to be too big, so we use wands," Parker answered and kept walking, wanting to get back to his original story.

"Sanger and Eisenhut were best friends, but the Sangers always owned the castle. Lord Eisenhut kept the name out of respect for Horatio Sanger," Parker explained.

Doug and Skip were a bit more taken aback than Pierce, who obviously knew about the wands and the history. Time to think was a bit of a luxury for them. The competition was scheduled for the following morning, and there was still a lot they didn't understand. Parker could tell, so he broke it down for them as simply as he could.

"See, the problem?," Parker began. "Ludicrous can't get in here.

And we can't get in Shadow Forest. That's why we have the Castle Cup this year. Some years are more important than others. The winners will be the team we know has the best chance of getting the Gem of Gicalma, the most powerful gem in Shadow Forest. If we can get that, then we can achieve all of our goals," Parker said mysteriously.

"What are the goals?" Doug asked.

"In due time. I've said too much," Parker answered.

"One more question," Doug asked.

Parker sort of rolled his eyes, but he understood that the new kids were probably filled with questions, and this was partly his job to answer them.

"One more," Parker answered.

"How did we swim in Toaster Pond in Waterville and end up in Sangerfield?" Parker was wondering how long it would take for Doug to come up with that question.

"Toaster Pond is a portal to Sangerfield. But you have to be gifted to make it through the portal. It doesn't work for just anyone."

"I'd prefer that to be the end of the questions though. I really want Eisenhut to be the one to answer any questions about the castle," Parker said.

"So who are the favorites tomorrow?" Skip interrupted.

Skip knew full well that there needed to be a change in conversation, but also that every competition had its favorites. The favorites were the ones that everyone thought could easily win the game. Skip was extremely competitive.

"You are," Parker said matter-of-factly.

Skip was quite happy about the fact that they were favorites. Doug and Pierce were concerned because the favorites for many competitions fell short of the expectations. They didn't want to fall short.

The three friends had been in Sangerfield for only a few hours, but were getting a great deal of information thrown at them.

"Where are we going now?" Doug said feeling a little winded from their walk. Which really wasn't the reason he was out of breath. It was the conversation that was knocking the wind out of him.

"We're going to meet Lord Eisenhut," Parker answered.

"After that we'll be going to establish your spot for the competition."

The four gifted teenagers came upon a large portrait of a man wearing a black robe with soft purple triangles on it. Doug quickly recognized the robe as being the same one the female referee had worn in Waterville. The man was handsome, had green eyes, and chiseled features. At the bottom of the very real looking portrait was the name, "**Lord Sanger**." Doug's mouth hung open, and he nudged Skip and pointed toward the nameplate.

Before Doug could compose himself, more strange events took place.

Parker looked at the portrait and said,

"Ingressus," and with that, the portrait moved to the side, and a hallway appeared.

"Quickly please," Parker said ushering the others into the hallway.

"What did you say to it?" Skip asked referring to the portrait.

"I said ingressus, which means enter in Latin," he explained.

Doug and Skip followed Pierce and Parker down the dark hallway toward Lord Eisenhut's study. They came to a huge door that had a new symbol on it. The doorknob was a simple vertical line. It looked like a big lower case l. Parker saw Doug and Skip staring at the odd looking doorknob.

"It means one or unity," Parker explained quickly.

He didn't want them preoccupied with the sign, so he cut to the chase.

"How do you know all this stuff?" Skip asked.

"I read a lot. Which you will do as well," Parker answered.

"Every symbol means something," Doug said quietly, but loud enough that everyone heard.

"Yes, there are symbols all around us. Only a few people care enough to learn about them. I find them interesting," Parker confided, and then banged on the door.

"Enter," a deep voice said. Doug recognized the voice from the dining hall, and he felt a little nervous walking in. The huge oak door slowly opened. Before the three teenagers stood Lord Eisenhut. No hair was out of place, which was very easy because he kept it very short. It was a hair cut Doug remembered a lot of men had during the Roman Empire. He had read about it in Mr. Acey's Social Studies class.

Eisenhut stood only a few inches taller than Doug, Skip and Pierce but was a bit shorter than Parker. His salt and pepper goatee was bushy but also well kept like his hair.

"Doug and Pierce. How nice to meet you," Eisenhut said slowly reaching out to shake the boy's hands one by one.

"I imagine you had some explaining to do," Eisenhut said to Pierce with a smile.

"Yes, sir, but it's alright now," Pierce answered, then looked at his two best friends.

"Right," he said waiting for an answer from Skip and Doug.

"Yes," they said slowly.

"And Skip, I like a girl with a nickname," Eisenhut said with a gentle grin.

"I'm Lord Eisenhut. Welcome," he said politely.

"You all understand why you're here," he said confidently.

They all shook their head yes. Although Doug and Skip were still getting used to the idea.

"Tomorrow morning will be the Hide-and-Seek competition. You are all quite good at it from what I hear."

The three friends couldn't help but be proud of their reputations.

"There will be a game of Hide-and-Seek in Gnome Field, which is the field you made it through this morning. The gnomes thrive on getting newcomers before they reach the castle," he said with caution.

"You didn't tell us about the gnomes," Doug said looking at Pierce.

"Hey, I'm pretty new to this whole thing too. I didn't know," he said trying to defend himself.

"You were fine. We had people watching to make sure you were safe," Eisenhut assured them.

"How did you see us?" Doug asked knowing full well that the lord had the gift, and was the most powerful person in Sangerfield.

"I know everything that goes on in Sangerfield. And my wife keeps me informed about Waterville," Eisenhut explained with a grin.

"The gnomes let you through because they knew we were expecting you. Luckily, it was before dark. Things change around here after dark," he warned.

"Gnomes," Doug asked looking as if he couldn't fully comprehend what he was hearing.

"Yes, tiny creatures who look like elves and are quite mean. And rather dangerous," Eisenhut explained. "They enjoy children but not to talk with, to eat," he said rather matter-of-factly. "Flesh seems to be their favorite part."

Doug, and Skip were chilled by the concept of man-eating gnomes.

"Why are we here, though? We can't be that good at Hide-and-

Seek, can we?" Skip said beginning to understand how important the competition was going to be.

"Ah," Lord Eisenhut sighed. "Yes, you are that good. I'm sure Parker told you that you are the favorites. You all have a keen sense of awareness for your surroundings. You'll need it tomorrow," he said "The winner tomorrow gets chosen to go into Shadow Forest to find the gems," Parker answered.

"It's quite an honor. It only happens once a year. It's not always quite as important a reason as it is this year. Actually, this is probably the most important year we have ever had, because we have special plans for the fall," Eisenhut answered seriously.

"What are the plans?" Doug asked beginning to put two and two together.

"The less you know, the more you will concentrate on tomorrow. I know you may have many questions regarding your...gift," he said slowly. But answers will all come after tomorrow's game," Eisenhut coached.

"If you have all of these teams, why can't we all go in to get the gems?" Skip asked as she brainstormed all of her options.

Lord Eisenhut smiled and said, "You are a smart one, Skip.

Unfortunately, Ludicrous isn't as aware if only a few go into the forest. More than that, she can close the cave off from everyone and we end up with nothing."

"Why does everyone in Waterville think you're dead?" Doug asked not completely believing the words exited his mouth.

"Not now," Parker jumped in.

"It's quite alright Parker. He deserves an explanation," Eisenhut said.

"It's easier to explain a death than it is to explain why someone is out of town so much. It came to a point where I needed to be here full-time, and my wife Ethel wanted to stay in Waterville to watch the pond," he explained.

"You three have had a long day. Go and find your confinement area for the Hide-and-Seek competition, and rest before the ceremonial dinner," Eisenhut suggested. "You will need a good meal and plenty of rest before the competition in the morning," he said.

And with that, he floated out of the room. The four left in the study looked at each other. "Let's go designate your prison," Parker suggested, and he led the three teens out the door, back down the hallway.

Chapter 3.2
Gnomes

"Gnomes are not typically friendly animals but they need us, so they'll cooperate tomorrow," Parker explained on their way out to choose a spot for the competition. "We feed them, and for that, they leave us alone. But we have an agreement that we will not enter their fields at night," he said.

"What's so special about the nighttime around here?" Skip asked. Parker looked for a moment like he was choosing his thoughts carefully.

"Just like the creatures in Shadow Forest, the Gnomes are extremely territorial. They have certain rituals they perform at night, and we need to respect that. They hate Ludicrous Zwevil as much as, or more than we do," he explained.

"Why?" Doug and Skip asked together.

"Ludicrous Zwevil tried to take over the fields a long time ago, and that didn't go over well with the gnomes. They're a rather angry lot, and they like to be left alone. They tolerate us, and we tolerate them," he said.

"There," Pierce said suddenly pointing to a clearing near a clump of a dozen trees.

"I think we should set down there," he suggested.

"Good choice," Parker complimented.

"I'm surprised no one claimed that area," Pierce said.

"Perhaps it was saved for you," Parker said with a smile.

At the same time, the sun was beginning to set and there was little time for more exploring in the fields, which made Skip and Doug happy. They enjoyed having their flesh attached to their bodies.

"It's getting dark. We need to move on," Parker warned.

In the distance the four travelers heard rumblings in the field of abnormally tall grass, and they saw smoke about fifty yards away. It was getting closer to them.

"Is that a fire?" Skip asked with a little fear in her voice.

"Sort of," Parker said. "They're looking to see who we are. We need to move a little faster before the sunsets, or they'll be having us for an appetizer," he said.

With that simple but dreadful statement, they began moving at a much faster pace. Behind them, each was looking to see if the parade of smoke and fire was catching up to them. Skip and Doug practically tripped over each other because they weren't paying attention to where they were walking.

As soon as they got to the gates, they felt a little safer. The gates swung open, and then closed quickly behind them. A loud thud was heard as the gates connected.

"What's to prevent them from coming in here?" Skip asked.

Parker looked at her and smiled with an evil grin, "They are forbidden to enter the castle. "They're territorial, but they're also afraid of the castle and it's immediate surroundings. We're very safe from everything in here. But we also have places of safety outside the castle grounds as well. You just need to stay away from Gnome Field and Shadow Forest."

Which was an ironic statement to make considering that those were two places that Doug, Skip and Pierce were most likely to see during their stay in Sangerfield, if the competition went well.

"We won't have to worry about the gnomes tomorrow. The Castle Cup is a sacred time for us. They won't mess with us if Lord Eisenhut is involved," Parker explained.

"Luckily, we have everything we need in here. You have not seen much of the castle, but there is much, much more," he said with a smile.

With that being said, the four teenagers entered the castle and made their way down the long hallway. Doug couldn't help but feel safe knowing that the huge gates, and Eisenhut's gift, were there to protect him and the rest of the guests at Sanger Castle.

"Why does it seem to get dark earlier here in the summer than at home?" Skip asked.

"Although it snows here and we get the four seasons, the daylight stays exactly the same every day of the year. The sun rises at 6 a.m. and sets at 7 p.m.," he said as they walked up a long staircase.

"We never got our room assignments," Doug remembered.

"You're fine. There was one reserved for you already," he said.

Feeling exhausted, Doug slowly climbed the stairs. Even though it seemed as though Parker and Lord Eisenhut answered a thousand questions, he knew he still had a thousand more. And knowing Skip, she had twice as many as that. "All in due time, all in due time," a voice kept saying in his head.

"All in due time," Skip said out loud.

Doug was dumbfounded by Skip's words. Perhaps his gift was getting stronger, or else it was merely a coincidence.

On the way up the stairs, Doug couldn't help but notice the moving pictures along the wall. All of the pictures were of three kids who looked liked they were around Doug's age. Doug pointed quietly toward the pictures. Each picture had a date on it and they spanned the past hundred years. Every step taken, they saw pictures with more recent dates. Recent meaning within the past fifty years. Doug, again saw the picture of someone he seemed to recognize but couldn't place the face. It almost looked like him but it was from twenty-two years previous. He glanced back, and then lost interest and kept walking. The whole situation was overwhelming.

"Who are in these pictures?" Skip asked.

"Those are the winners of all of the Hide-and-Seek competitions Sanger Castle has ever had. None, however, are as important as this year," Parker said. "Lord Eisenhut has ambitious ideas for the Castle this year. Let's just see how tomorrow goes," he continued.

When they reached the top floor overlooking the ceramic floors of the hallway one hundred feet below, they came to a door, which had the same symbol as Eisenhut's door.

"Unity," Doug thought to himself.

"Insluipen," Parker commanded, and the door slowly opened.

"What does that mean," Skip asked.

"It's Dutch for enter," Parker answered. Knowing Skip would have another question, he looked at her with a grin, "You don't expect us to always use Latin do you?"

Skip suddenly wanted to know every language, and was a little worried the kids walking around the castle were a lot smarter than she was. The view of the room greeted their eyes, and the suite that appeared before them amazed Doug, Skip, and Pierce.

There was a sitting room, with a black leather sectional sofa, and a white leather chair that was more comfortable than it looked. Skip sat down in the white chair feeling tired from the day.

In the corner of the room was a fireplace that did not need to be lit, because it was Summer time, and a compact disc player that held ten cd's. In addition, there were six surround sound speakers that were quite small. Pierce couldn't help himself and pressed play. The sound that came out was unlike they have ever heard, so clear and crisp. They looked at the compact disk case that leaned against the wall. It had every cd that the three teenagers ever wanted. Classical music was playing on the CD player at the moment, and classical was not Skip and Pierce's favorite.

"Fritz Kreisler," Parker said.

"Who?" Doug asked, sort of enjoying the music.

"Fritz Kreisler is the composer. You'll get used to it. Eisenhut loves classical music," Parker said whispering to the three as if he was letting them in on a big secret.

"Where's the television?" Doug asked in wonder.

"There isn't one," said a soft British voice.

Pierce turned around as a woman of about sixty was walking into the room.

"And don't plan on turning the stereo up either. It has a governor on it," the woman said.

"What's a governor?" Skip asked.

"It's a device that stops it from getting too loud," Parker explained before the woman had a chance.

The three Waterville residents stared at the woman as she made her way around the room, as if she was inspecting it.

"I am Baroness Choukeir," said the petite blond woman who entered the suite.

"You must be Doug and Pierce. It's nice to meet you," she said shaking their hands firmly knowing whom each boy was "And you must be Skip," she said with a warm smile.

The three newcomers said hello.

"What do you do here?" Skip asked.

"I am the Resident Director of Exodus Wing, which is where you are right now. And to answer your former question more directly, there isn't a television because we don't want children watching t.v, it's too violent," she said in disgust. "Music is good for the imagination. Especially classical music," and with that, Pierce and Skip gave each other a look of repulsion.

Doug, however, enjoyed the thought of classical music. It made him feel older, more mature. Although his newfound gift was helping his maturity.

"However, music cannot be played during the hours of 4 – 8 p.m. And lights out at 10 pm." She said directly to Pierce.

"But it's summer," Skip argued. Although in Waterville she would have to get up early the next morning to milk the cows. So staying up late was never a high priority for her.

"Yes, well, rules are rules," Choukeir retorted. "And plus, you have a game tomorrow," she reminded them.

"What if it rains?" Doug asked.

"Then you get wet," she said with her right eyebrow raised.

Skip loved the idea of playing in the rain. Doug and Pierce didn't care either way. They both just wanted to win.

"Skip, your bedroom is in there, and boys you are the other. The lavatory is there. It has both a shower and a bathtub," she said.

Pierce and Doug walked quickly to check out their room for the evening. Simultaneously jumping on their beds to check the comfort level. They were more comfortable than any bed they had ever slept on. No lumps. Both of the large, warm down quilts that covered the beds were maroon, which must have been the choice color for everything in the suite, because the shades were maroon as well.

Each bed was queen size, with four pillows. The bathroom had a large gray marble floor that flowed through it, and a huge mirror on the wall over the sink. The counter around the sink had three sections, and each one was labeled for each one of the guests.

They walked back through to the bedroom, and Pierce found himself curious to look out at the night sky in Sangerfield. He came upon a window, and looked out one of the four sections of the pane. The sky was turning pink, and there were no clouds to be seen.

Pierce kept looking around, noticing that something seemed different. Then he realized what it was. There wasn't a stone wall around the field, like normal it was completely open. He could see mountains in the distance and the forest over to his right. Baroness Choukeir could sense Pierce's wonder.

"Where is the wall?" he asked.

"Hmmm..." she began, as if choosing her words carefully.

"Those windows are special. They show you the best Sangerfield has to offer, without the barriers that work against us," Choukeir said prophetically.

"What do you mean?" Pierce asked her, feeling confused.

"We don't want to always concentrate on the barriers that guard us, such as the front gates to the castle, or Gnome Field, which can be very dangerous. So the best parts of Sangerfield are all you can see. We call them our Rose-colored Windows," she explained.

Pierce, Skip and Doug didn't totally get what she meant, but it had been a long day, and they weren't sure if they were going to fully understand her meaning anyway, so they decided to drop the conversation.

"I will let you adapt to your surroundings. I know you have had a long and surprising day. Dinner will be served in one hour. Please be punctual. Lord Eisenhut does not like it when one is tardy," she said. She began to walk out, and then quickly turned around.

"It is an honor to have you staying in the Exodus Wing," and then she turned and walked out the large wooden double doors. The three looked at each other in wonder. Being the favorites and having it be an honor to be in their presence, was a lot to handle.

"Now that we're alone, I have some questions," Doug said looking at Pierce. In return, Pierce seemed to have been anticipating the moment and couldn't wait to open up.

"Why...What...How?" Doug found himself unable to speak.

"How long have you known?" Skip chimed in trying to speak for her tongue-tied cousin.

"I guess I've known for awhile. I mean my dad always had odd photographs around the house. Once I walked into the kitchen and he and my mom were making dinner without using pots or pans. They had wands in their hands."

Doug and Skip were taking the whole conversation in. Both were finding themselves a little more relaxed. The black leather sectional helped, as did Fritz Kreisler's composition they were listening to.

"I spent too much time reading about being gifted, and Sanger Castle, letting my studies in school go, which is why I almost failed last year," Pierce confided.

"I mean we're all good at something. What I was good at they just didn't teach n school. At least, public school," Pierce let on.

"Is that the boarding school my parents were talking about," Doug said out loud.

"It's early, and we have a lot to worry about. Please don't say anything, but our challenge is really important," Pierce said getting more excited as he spoke.

"What's going on," Skip asked referring to Doug's question.

"My parents said they were going to send me to a boarding school if everything worked out. They meant here, didn't they," Doug asked looking at Pierce.

"Most likely. Your parents are gifted too," Pierce said.

"And yours are too," he said looking at Skip.

Although they were surprised, they always knew their parents were a little odd. Living on a farm was hard work, but some of the chores always seemed to get done without anyone lifting a finger. Skip always remembered hearing some of her other friends who lived on farms complain about milking cows, and feeding horses, and cleaning the barn.

Fortunately for Skip, her barn seemed to be self-cleaning. Her dad would walk in to clean it, and come out a minute later saying it was done. Skip checked to see if her father could clean that quickly, and the barn was always completely spotless. She just figured her father was a fast cleaner.

Doug stared around the room and began to feel comfortable and safe. Never in his wildest dreams did he think he would live in such a cool looking space. It was better than anything he ever got for his birthday.

Unable to hold in his excitement, he sort of burst out, "Have you ever seen a room so cool before in your life? Everything is state of the art!"

"And we're in a castle," Skip said looking around, still in awe of her surroundings.

Doug began to walk around the room and touch everything. He seemed to be taking it all in piece by piece.

While Doug was looking at everything and Skip was resting in her chair, something fell behind them. Pierce turned around, and a leather bound folder opened with rules and regulations to the Castle Cup Hide-and-Seek Competition.

"Did that folder just open on it's own?" Skip asked.

"It certainly looked that way," Doug answered.

"What is it?" Skip asked.

"It looks like a rule book for the Hide-and-Seek game tomorrow," Pierce said holding it in his hand.

"Considering weather doesn't matter tomorrow, we better look at this," Doug suggested.

All three teenagers looked at the leather bound folder together. Everything on it was written in script, and it looked very formal.

Castle Cup
Hide-and-Seek Competition
Where: Gnome Field
When: Saturday Morning
Time: 8:00 a.m. (Dusk) **13 &14** year olds only
Who: Three person teams. Positions are as follows.
Hunter: Pierce Butterworth
Seeker: Doug Manion
Guard: Skip Corbin

Boundaries:
North through the field to North Marker (Blue Marker on Big Pine Tree)
South Castle Border
West To Toaster Pond
East to Shadow Forest Border – DO NOT GO INTO THE FOREST

Rules
Seekers stand at the tree and slowly count to twenty. Seeker's job is to catch as many hiders as possible. Seekers cannot tag other Seekers but do have to wear team flags.

Guards stand around their confinement. Guards are able to leave their prisons to protect their seekers, but if they leave their prisons unattended, other guards can free the captured prisoners already in their possession.

Guards have the ability to tag Seekers and Hiders. They are allowed to do anything to protect their team and confinement area.

Hiders wear their team flag and hide from the seekers. The Hider's job is to find the hidden Gem of Ashleigh, and get it back to safety without getting caught.

First hider to get to safety with the gem wins. Any Hider caught by a Seeker in the process will have to give the Gem of Ashleigh to the referee to hide again.

Game ends when the Gem of Ashleigh is found.

Sudden Death
If the gem is not found in one hour, the team with the most prisoners captured, wins.

"What is the Gem of Ashleigh?" Skip asked looking at Pierce hoping he would know.

"Read the bottom," he said pointing.

"You can do the honors," Skip answered sarcastically.

Pierce smiled and focused on the words written in script on the leather bound folder.

"Ashleigh is a flower that can only be found in Sangerfield. The gem forms under the flowers when they grow up three at a time, which isn't very common. It doesn't have a lot of power, but it is considered very beautiful," Pierce read.

Doug and Skip were still a little freaked out by Pierce's knowledge even though he was reading from the book. But they were happy that he was so smart when it came to Sangerfield and the castle. Not to mention being gifted. Without him they would be lost.

"Does anything seem strange to you about those rules?" Skip asked inquisitively.

"No," Doug and Pierce answered together.

"Nothing," Skip prodded.

"No," Doug answered again.

Out of the three friends, Skip was the one with the critical eye. Not that she was critical, but she paid close attention to directions and rules. Skip pointed to the time the game was played, a little annoyed that she had to point out an obvious mistake in the rules.

"How can it be dusk at 8 a.m.?" Parker said to himself, if it's light by six.

"Mother Nature is taking a back seat to the competition. This is serious," Pierce said flatly.

The music ended and the clock began to chime seven times, which meant it was time to make their way to the dining hall for dinner.

"We'd better go. I don't want to be late and have Eisenhut angry with me," Doug said.

Skip and Pierce agreed.

As they walked to the dining hall, they talked strategy.

They followed the long staircase, down to the main hallway with the pictures displayed, including the one that was covered by the black cloth. Other teenage competitors walked toward the dining hall. Doug and Pierce were the type of boys that could smell out food, so they weren't worried about getting lost on the way to dining hall.

Once there, they saw hundreds of teenagers sitting at three long tables. Eisenhut, Doha, and Choukeir were sitting at the head table together, which was on a stage and was about thirty feet long. The table appeared to be solid oak, with long oak benches that the adults sat on.

As the three walked in, all the adult robed icons of the castle nodded their heads as if to say hello to the three newcomers. Eisenhut gave a slight smile to Doug.

Doug, Pierce, and Skip walked over to open spots at one of the tables. Two boys and a girl turned and said hello.

"Hello," Skip said in return.

Thinking they could use a few friends in this strange new place, she also wanted to feel out the competition.

"This is Colin Bollock," the British accented girl said, pointing to a blonde-haired boy with glasses standing next to her. "This is Patricia Skiba," she said pointing to the other girl, who was nearly six feet tall.

"And I'm Valeo, Joanne Valeo" she said very Bond-like with a smile. Standing no more than five feet tall, Valeo had flaming red hair.

"We heard you're great at Hide-and-Seek," she said matter-of-factly.

"How do you know?" Skip asked curiously.

"It's a pretty small place, although it looks huge. People talk.

Especially them," she said gesturing toward a team of three wearing red shirts.

"Who are they?" Skip asked with a grimace, already being able to tell that she wasn't going to like them. The red-shirted kids were the ones walking out of the gate the day the Waterville natives arrived.

"That's Jian," she said pointing out the dark haired Asian boy.

"That's his sister Mae," pointing toward the female equivalent of her brother. Mae had long black hair, compared to Jian's short black hair. "And that's Ngai," Valeo said referring to the boy with bleach blonde hair sitting next to Mae and Jian.

Skip spent a lot of time staring around the room with her mouth wide open. "Where are all of these kids from?" she asked.

"All over the world, of course," Valeo answered. "We're from London, as are many teams, but pretty much every nation is represented here," she said.

"How do they speak?" she said feeling stupid for asking the question.

" I mean not everyone in the world speaks English," she added quickly before Valeo could answer.

"Good question. However, everyone here does. In order to come here you have to speak English fluently. It's a prerequisite for the preliminaries," Valeo explained.

"What preliminaries?" Doug asked.

"The competition you were in yesterday," Valeo answered referring to the championship match in Waterville. The one that two of the three kids thought was just another neighborhood game.

Doug and Skip were still in awe that so many people knew they were coming. But mostly they were amazed by the fact that all of this had happened to them in the past twenty-four hours.

"We got word from our judges yesterday that you would be here.

You see, you three are the only gifted ones who have never been trained professionally in Hide-and-Seek," she began explaining.

Doug and Skip looked at each other in wonder at the idea that you could be trained in Hide-and-Seek. The gifted thing was still something to get used to. Valeo could read the thought on their faces.

"Waterville has had more competitors than any other place in the world, so they don't get trained. It's natural to be good, even great players, for you guys," she continued as they walked and sat down at one of the large medieval tables.

"Not everyone in Waterville is gifted though, right?" Doug

asked…anyone who could answer.

"No, not everyone. But there are key families in Waterville that are," Pierce said.

"Like whom?" Skip jumped in.

"I really don't know. My dad wouldn't tell me," Pierce said, "But there are others."

"We also understand that Lord Eisenhut is from Waterville, so that makes you guys a little more advanced in popularity than the rest of us," Valeo said with a bit of envy.

Eisenhut stood up and clapped his hands three times. Suddenly, four men with bagpipes came out of each wall that surrounded the dining hall. A loud, long, low horn sound began flowing through the air, and everyone watched as the men began playing bagpipes.

"Lord Eisenhut loves bagpipes," Valeo quickly explained.

"Why?" Skip asked as if she didn't like the noise very much.

"He believes they signify the beginning, or the end of something special. Depending on when they're played," Valeo explained.

"So is this the beginning, or the end," Doug asked.

"It's very much the beginning," Valeo answered.

The bagpipers walked around the room until they met up with each other. Forming a single file line, as quickly as they appeared out of the walls, they walked back through one together. This single file line signified the importance of being a team. Doug, Pierce, and Skip were clearly impressed by the show.

"There's more," Valeo assured.

"Most nights are like this," she said.

"How long have you been here?" Skip asked.

"All summer," Valeo said.

"Have you guys been practicing all summer?" Pierce asked.

"Yes," she said.

The other three were sure they were not as prepared as everyone else in the room. Regardless, whether they WERE the favorites, and FROM the town that produced the best Hide-and-Seek players in the world. It was easy to feel intimidated. When they looked around the room, they realized that the other teams sole purpose all summer was to win tomorrow's competition.

Suddenly Eisenhut clapped his hands again, and immediately everyone's focus was directed at him. As soon as he held their attention, (which he was very good at getting), he said in his deep voice, "Let dinner begin."

Food, like magic, appeared on the table, as well as the place settings to put it on. There was an array of huge turkeys and pasta. Foods that Doug had never seen before appeared next to him, and all the kids took their turns putting it on their plates.

"This is amazing!" Skip said with a lot of excitement in her voice.

Doug began eating his dinner, finding himself famished after all the excitement. The lights dimmed when everyone was still eating, and the crowd, "oohed," when it happened.

"Let's make the best of it, shall we?" Eisenhut said standing up.

He clapped his hands three times again. Doha and Choukeir smiled at the newcomers in the crowd, as if they knew something unexpected was going to happen.

Men and women in long black robes walked into the dining hall, and they were all carrying folded shirts in their arms. At the same time that everyone looked up, Skip looked down at the table. The food, silverware, and plates all had been cleaned up without any of the children lifting a finger.

"I have GOT to learn how to do this at home," Skip thought to herself.

The people in the robes seemed to be floating through the air. And one familiar looking woman floated over towards Skip, Doug, and Pierce. The closer she got, the further Skip and Doug's jaws dropped open. Pierce was feeling at ease knowing the last thing he was holding back from his friends, was now out in the open.

"Gram," Skip and Doug said together, as they looked up at the short woman hovering a few inches above the floor.

"Hi Dad," Pierce said to the robed man who floated along with Corbin Gram.

Chapter 3.3
Long Lost Relatives

Corbin Gram and Dr. Butterworth were standing in front of the three teenagers. Pierce felt the guard that he kept up all day drop like a heavy weight. All of his secrets were no longer kept deep inside of him.

"These are your jerseys for tomorrow," Corbin Gram and Dr. Butterworth said together handing the three kids hunter green shirts.

Skip and Doug didn't know if they wanted to cry or laugh as they stared at their grandmother. They also didn't realize that Pierce had known she was alive. A handsome man in his early fifties, standing almost six feet tall was standing with her. Skip and Doug knew it was Pierce's dad. He was an imposing figure, with dark black hair, and he wore round wire rimmed glasses.

There was no denying that Corbin Gram was actually standing in front of them as well. She was about five feet tall, with white hair, a soft round face, and also wore wire-rimmed glasses that looked like something Ben Franklin would have worn in the 1700's.

"Hello, son," Pierce's Dad said.

Pierce stood up and gave him a hug. Skip and Doug were hugging their very undead grandmother tightly as well. They were afraid to let go, fearing it might be a dream.

"I'm sorry you two, but it was the only way we could do it," she explained.

"What do you mean," Doug asked holding back his tears.

"I'm staying on here. No one would have believed I was moving out of town, so your parents thought I should pass away, if you know what I mean," she explained.

"So they DO know," Skip and Doug said together.

"Yes, they know," she confided. Doug realized he misunderstood the conversation his parents were having regarding Corbin Gram. When they said they were going to miss her, they meant because she moved to Sangerfield, not because she was dead.

"Why is all of this happening now?" Doug asked.

Skip definitely wanted to know the answer too.

"Because," Corbin Gram began. "You show more maturity when you become a teenager. It's a rite of passage, and this is the reward for taking that responsibility seriously," she explained.

"But now, unfortunately, the castle and your gift are at risk. We need the gem from Shadow Forest," Dr. Butterworth said gravely. "The competition is taking place at the right time. And this year is more important than ever. We'd like to continue our plans to make this a boarding school for the gifted. And we hope that it will be up to you to get the Gem of Gicalma so we can do it." he said. "We'll walk you back to your suite," Pierce's Dad suggested, staring intently at his son.

Leaving the crowd of children, they all noticed that Eisenhut gave them a fatherly wink. They smiled warmly back to him, Doug and Skip were a little red in the cheeks from the whole experience. The sound of their feet against the ceramic floor didn't seem to make a noise. Although there were over one hundred kids conversing behind them, Doug was unable to hear a sound. Everything seemed to be going so fast, that it was happening in slow motion. Dr. Butterworth and Corbin Gram were speaking, but Doug could only concentrate on his grandmother's lips and her chubby cheeks that bounced as she walked. Doug couldn't believe that his grandmother was walking right next to him.

"Focus," was all he could think to himself, and that was all he

needed to wake up, and be a part of the conversation. "Gram, you came here this week," Doug asked.

"Yes, I came through the pond with Duncan and Lord Eisenhut," she answered.

On their way back to their suite, Corbin Gram explained how Lord Eisenhut put a spell over her to make people think she passed on during the wake, and then as soon as the people left to go to Doug's house, she met up with him at the pond. The unannounced storm almost ruined the whole plan.

"So was that you who was calling to me in the hallway the night of your wake," Doug asked remembering the fateful evening.

"Yes," Corbin Gram answered, a little embarrassed.

Eisenhut wasn't very happy with her for that little stunt.

"Did you send me the Book of Spells?" Skip asked her grandmother.

"Yes, I thought you might recognize my handwriting," she said.

The doors to the suite opened in front of them when Corbin Gram said "Insluipen" and all five people entered.

"Have a seat, we need to talk with you," they said seriously.

"How do you like your rooms?" Corbin Gram asked, trying to break the ice.

"They're better than home," Doug answered quickly.

"Nothing is better than home, but I know what you mean," Corbin Gram corrected and winked at him.

"Baroness Choukeir wanted to make sure you had everything you needed, so I helped design the room for you. I'm glad you like it," she said.

Dr. Butterworth started the conversation, so he could explain everything that was riding on the three teens from Waterville.

"We want to create a boarding school that is both highly competitive with any school in the world, but is also fun and magical, like school should be," he explained.

"A place where we can practice all levels of Science, including being gifted. Here we can teach about herbs, spells, but also biology and anatomy. Not just of humans either," Corbin Gram said with a grin as if holding back something.

Doug and Skip couldn't help but notice that their grandmother was much more serious than she had ever been in their presence, and they knew that they had the potential to be a part of an important mission.

"Once you turn eighteen, you have to move on to college, but you will have many choices where that is concerned," Butterworth said coyly.

"However, without the gems, there won't be a school in the fall," Gram confided.

"If that happens, what will happen to all of you?" Pierce asked.

"I'm not sure, but I know we won't be able to go home," his father answered.

"Why?" Doug asked knowing full-well why his grandmother couldn't go home.

"I didn't leave under perfect circumstances," Dr. Butterworth began. "Some colleagues at the college saw me, well... let me say, they saw me using my gift. I was planning on leaving anyway but the situation made it a little more dire," he explained.

At that moment, Pierce, Skip, and Doug realized that the competition had gotten more serious.

"We need to say goodnight. It will be lights out in about twenty minutes. Don't forget to brush your teeth...for two minutes," Gram reminded them. They couldn't believe how quickly the time flew by, and none of the three had a desire to fall asleep.

"We'll see you in the morning at the competition," Dr. Butterworth said giving his son a kiss goodnight. Corbin Gram did the same to her two grandchildren.

"We'll be rooting for you," she said to the three teenagers who were feeling happy at seeing their long lost family members.

However, they were discontented at the thought of not seeing them again if the gem wasn't taken from Shadow Forest. The Castle Cup was merely a preliminary, but one they had to win. All three wanted to be the ones to enter Shadow Forest.

The two adults floated out the doorway. The door locked from the inside behind them, although none of the three left inside had locked it.

"We have got to win the Castle Cup tomorrow," Pierce said with fervor.

Skip, Doug and Pierce got ready for bed, making sure that their alarms were set for 6:30 a.m. Strangely enough, their alarms were already set. Although they didn't feel overly tired, they quickly fell asleep as their heads hit the pillow on their new comfortable beds.

All three slept through the night dreaming about the day before. Although they experienced the same day, it was different for each one. One grandparent, who was thought to be dead, was alive and well. Skip and Doug could not believe that the grandmother they thought they lost forever, was very much alive and extremely important in the life she now took part in full-time.

The night was quiet. Inside the walls that surrounded the castle, was the safest place in the world to be. Right outside the guarded fortress was the most dangerous place that anyone could ever imagine. The gnomes, being nocturnal, searched for trouble and despair. The creatures that lived in the forest took turns during the night and day to keep watch over their land. One with the dark gift controlled the forest, evil gnomes controlled the field, and the strongest controls the castle. All could not be any different.

At 6:30 in the morning, the three children in Suite 62, who had the same dreams, heard very different wake up calls.

"Wake up, wake up, sleepy head. Get up, get up, and get out of bed," was the alarm the Skip woke to.

"GET OUT OF BHED. WHAT'S WRONG WITH YA LADDIE? DO YOU NEED ME TO COME OVER THERE AND PULL THE COVERS OWHT FROM UNDER YA!!!" was the wake up that Pierce heard, although that was not the one he chose.

"I have GOT to learn how to set that alarm," he said out loud.

No sooner did he get the words out, when he heard laughter coming from the clock.

"Ur' father changed tha one ya set. He taught you would like dat one betta," the alarm said laughing.

"You talk," Pierce said, as Doug was waking up.

"Ov curse I talk," it said, back in a thick Scottish brogue.

"Do you have a name?" Pierce asked, quickly, coming out of his fog, not believing he was talking to an alarm clock.

"Sebastian," it answered.

"And dat iz me broder Edgar," he said, shining a light out of his side toward Doug's alarm clock.

"Hello, Laddies, how do you do?" Edgar answered, in an equally deep Scottish brogue.

"This is so weird," Doug thought. Talking alarms clocks. It was a lot to get used to.

"You both better be gettin ready for the competition. It's a big day…yes laddies, a big day," the alarms clocks said in unison.

After all three got ready and met in the common room, they talked about the dreams they all had about the competition. Pierce was distracted thinking about his new talking alarm clock.

"Does your alarm clock talk?" Pierce asked Skip, interrupting her as she was explaining her dream.

"Yes, I noticed that last night. She began talking to me," Skip answered, trying not to be annoyed by Pierce's interruption.

"She," Doug asked.

"Of course, I get a female alarm clock. Her name is Isabel," Skip answered.

"Does she have an accent?" Pierce asked.

"An accent," Skip asked looking at Doug, as if she thought Pierce was going out of his mind.

"Ours are from Scotland or England or something," Pierce explained.

Skip once again turned to Doug who gave her a look to let her know that Pierce was quite serious. "No, mine doesn't have an accent," Skip said.

The more she thought of it, however, she realized that not too many people would believe she had a talking alarm clock, so perhaps the boys weren't exaggerating about their alarm clocks with accents.

As the three walked out the doors, the lock made a noise behind them. All three of them realized that their mindset had to turn from being teenagers to competitors; if they wanted to end the game the same way they were beginning the game as the favorites.

The long trip down the spiral staircase seemed to take forever. All three of them could feel the butterflies in their stomachs. Their nerves were going haywire now, but would subside when the game began. At least, that's what they hoped. Pierce, the most competitive of all, had his game face on, and he was ready to go.

Chapter 4.0
Castle Cup

O nce they made their way to the enormous dining hall, all three noticed that the tables were no longer in the three medieval settings from dinner. They were now separated into triangular tables that seated three.

"How do they do that?" Skip wondered aloud.

"They must be different tables than last night," Pierce said as if he knew the answer, although he didn't. Some things magical just couldn't be explained.

Teams were sitting around the tables talking strategy for the competition. Dr. Butterworth walked up behind the three teammates.

"Eat lightly this morning. You don't want anything heavy in your stomachs. And bring fruit to put in your backpacks," he suggested.

"We don't have backpacks Dad," Pierce said looking at his father, wondering if he had forgotten to grab the backpacks.

"Don't worry. They'll be given to you before you leave the dining hall. All teams get them after breakfast so no cheating occurs," his father answered putting a hand on his son's shoulder. "I'll see you out there. Good luck," he said with a slow wink as he strolled off toward Eisenhut's direction.

"You guys must think you're something hot," one boy said with a heavy Asian accent.

Pierce, Skip, and Doug looked at each other, and didn't have to turn around to see who it was. Pierce was not in the mood to deal with an arrogant teenager before the competition.

"No, not really," Doug answered, feeling very calm.

"I'm Doug. This is Skip, and.." Doug started to introduce himself.

"We know who you are. Everyone thinks you're the favorites," Jian answered. "We won the past two years, and we don't plan on losing today," he said and turned and walked away.

All three looked at each other wondering what they did wrong.

Valeo walked by laughing a little.

"I see you met Jian," she said sarcastically.

"What's his problem?" Skip asked.

"They're sort of competitive without any sportsmanship," Skiba answered. It was the first time the tall thirteen year-old spoke.

"They're obnoxious, but you just need to get to know them," Valeo answered. "They're also extremely fast and quiet, so look out for them. They're looking to tag you first," she warned.

Before she could give any more advice, she was interrupted. Lord Eisenhut stood up and clapped his hands three times as he always did when he wanted the full attention of everyone in the crowd. Everyone instantly stopped what they were doing. The kids unlucky enough to be walking around, made their way quickly to their seats.

"Good morning," he said loudly to everyone.

Everyone said good morning in return.

"We will be making our way to the fields in the next few minutes.

You all received your rules. Your backpacks will be given to you as you exit the dining hall. We will be handing them out in a timely fashion, so be quick after you get them," he suggested strongly. "I know I don't have to remind you how important this competition is. The team that gets the Gem of Ashleigh wins. If Sudden Death occurs, the team with the most captures wins. However, we prefer you find the gem." He said as a matter of extreme importance. "Please make your way to get your leather packs, and we will all meet in Gnome Field in thirty minutes," he said, and then turned around and floated off the stage area. The two Barons and the professors followed him out the door. Dr. Butterworth gave Doug, Skip, and Pierce one last wink for good luck.

Skip, Pierce, and Doug stood up and left to get their packs. Jian and his team were behind them.

"I plan on tagging them first," Jian said to Mae and Ngai, although it was really directed toward Doug.

Pierce turned around and got in Jian's face, eyes glaring into his. Fists clenched, but feeling very calm. Skip and Doug were ready to pull him away, but they knew Pierce would practice restraint.

"We'll do our talking out on the field," was all Pierce said, and he quickly turned around. Jian didn't say another word.

Pierce grabbed the leather pack with their names on it and walked out. He put his finger to his lips to tell Doug and Skip not to say anything until they were allowed some privacy. Doug was hoping to tune in some voices to help him during the competition. Skip was just hoping she would have to guard Jian and his teammates.

They made their way down the hallway, gazing at the pictures of all the teams that came before them. Doug took one last glance at the photo that looked so familiar to him, and then he realized why. It was the same picture he found in an old box of photos last year that his Dad had saved. When Doug asked his father what they were, he made up a story that they were from his little league baseball days. Doug had noticed at the time that the picture didn't involve baseball, and there were only three people in the photograph. Not enough players for a baseball team. Skip's Dad was one of the three in the photo, and Pierce's Dad was the third.

"Look at the photo," Doug said stopping Pierce and Skip.

Their mouths dropped.

"That's my Dad," Skip said surprisingly.

"That's my Dad," Pierce announced.

"They won before," Doug said.

"They won more than once," Pierce answered. "They are the only team to have won four times in a row. And the only reason why they didn't win five is that they were too old to play anymore," he pointed out.

Doug suddenly felt confused. "But my dad told me that he used to play with my Uncle Bill and some girl named Nancy."

"My dad met your parents here during the summer, which is why he moved to Waterville with my grandparents," Pierce explained.

"What happened to Nancy?" Skip asked.

"I guess she moved away," Pierce explained.

As their gaze widened, the other three-team pictures came into focus.

"They all played the same positions that we do," Pierce said having just found out a few weeks earlier.

"A little more pressure for the three of us today," Doug said with a deep breath.

"We have two ways to go about this," Pierce said.

He had the full attention of his two teammates. "We can focus on getting prisoners, or we can focus on the gem," he said.

"In that case, we have three," Skip announced. "I say we focus on grabbing prisoners when we can, AND look for the Gem. The way we always do it," she said confidently.

"Good idea," Doug answered focusing on his inner voices, or something else that would edge out the competition.

"I'll look for people to pick off," Pierce said seriously.

"I'll get the gem," Doug said.

"I won't take a chance of leaving my spot," Skip said. "I just want to guard who's there."

It looked like a swarm of colors walking out to the field. Some of the teams had stripes and others had solid colors. Others had patterns and shapes all over their shirts, but none of the hundreds of teams wore the same colors.

The oddest thing about the situation was the fact that it was getting dark outside as the minutes clicked by. It should have been getting lighter, as the morning was drifting towards day.

"The Eisenhut Effect," Doug thought out loud.

"What's that?" Pierce asked looking like he was ready for battle.

Pierce and Skip were the true competitors of the three. Their shoulders lifted a bit, and Pierce imagined how it must have been for a gladiator to walk into battle. Doug felt confident, but something about competition always scared him a bit.

"Eisenhut Effect's, a little name I came up with to explain why things here happen differently than they do in Waterville," Doug explained.

Skip and Pierce laughed a bit, which calmed their nerves before the big competition.

"Look at that," Skip said, observing one lone crow flying through the air. No other birds were flying in the dark morning sky.

"Isn't it odd that that is the only bird we can see," Skip said. Pierce shrugged his shoulders, ready to focus on Hide-and-Seek.

"At least we know they have regular animals here along with the magical ones," Doug said feeling a bit more himself.

The crow flew in a circular pattern over the competition that was getting ready to begin. Skip felt a chill for some reason. She wasn't sure if it was from the untimely flying crow, or the competition. A stage was set up, and Baron Doha and Choukeir were standing on it, next to many other barons and professors.

"The Barons are in maroon, and the professors are in black," Valeo said as she walked by the three newcomers.

The color the professors and barons chose to wear seemed to be the opposite of what they had worn the day before, because Eisenhut was wearing maroon. Although, they guessed that Eisenhut could wear whatever color he wanted on any day he chose.

Eisenhut looked in the sky every so often and caught a glimpse of the crow. He spoke loudly, so he could get everyone's attention.

"You have the rules. Remember what I said in the dining hall. The Gem trumps all other captures. And remember. You may use your gift during the game, which should make it interesting," he said, amusing himself and the other barons. "There are lookouts watching your every move. Impress them a bit if you can," he said seriously in jest.

All the competitors seemed to be a bit offended by his concern with cheating, but Doug was happy that there were safeguards to make sure that no one even considered being dishonest.

"And yes, one more thing," he continued. "The Gem of Ashleigh is to be considered sacred and powerful. Nothing that powerful is easy to get. You may look and look, and look you'll do. But find it where they're standing two." As he made the announcement, Doug noticed the unknown female judge from their game in Waterville.

He quietly pointed in her direction, and Pierce and Skip looked.

"Gail Naylor is her name. She is a GT…gifted and talented," Pierce explained. Doug and Skip looked a bit confused. "She's very smart," Pierce said in laymen's terms.

"And she's highly respected here," Valeo said before she walked away.

Doug seemed satisfied with the answer and went back to focusing on Eisenhut's rhyme. He wasn't a big fan of riddles.

The referees were looking at Skip, Doug and Pierce at the same time. Then they turned and walked away without an expression on their face. Doug got goose bumps seeing them again. The game was likely to be unlike anything he had ever experienced, but he also realized that his two partners were ready for the new challenge that lay ahead. And so was he.

Looking up into the sky, Doug saw dark clouds begin slowly rolling in.

"We're going to get wet," Doug told him teammates.

"Oh yeah," Pierce agreed feeling very psyched.

"Good," Skip said, "some of these guys won't be able to handle getting wet."

"Do you ever get the feeling she's tougher than we are?" Doug asked Pierce.

Pierce just nodded his head in agreement. With all of the banter back and forth about the weather, he felt a feeling of calmness come over him, which was odd because he usually got nervous before a competition.

"All guards to their posts," Lord Eisenhut announced, looking up toward the clouds as the rain began to fall.

"Well, that's me," Skip said taking a deep breath looking at Doug and Pierce.

"Good luck," Doug said to her.

"Yeah, you guys too," she said back.

Skip walked away toward the open field with a smile her face. Her forest green shirt disappeared into the tall grass.

"You ready to do this?" Pierce asked Doug when they were alone together.

"Yeah," Doug answered, feeling psyched and a little wet all at the same time.

He had never been much of an athlete, but it was never too late to become one, and this was the perfect time.

"Remember, watch my back, but look for the Gem of Ashleigh," Pierce offered as advice.

"Gotcha," Doug answered.

"Seekers, get ready to run," Eisenhut gave as his next command. "I'll see you out there," Doug said softly.

"Not if we see you first," Jian answered walking by.

Like the crow, Jian seemed to be circling Doug and Pierce, and it was as intimidating as he wanted it to be.

"He wasn't talking with you," Pierce said with an angry tone.

Mae and Ngai were already gone, so Pierce was hoping Skip would somehow get Jian out of the way first. Jian had much the same thought about Pierce.

As soon as the Seekers were out of sight, Eisenhut began counting slowly to ten, and then blew the horn. He looked up and saw the lone crow flying above.

At the same time he blew the horn, the sky began to darken a little more. Torches were lit around the bridge, and at the top of every team's post. The now heavy rain didn't seem to dampen the fires.

Pierce took off running, ready for battle. Jian ran behind him to see if Pierce was going to catch up with Doug. The number one goal of every team was to knock out the favorites first. Pierce suddenly closed his eyes and began to hover above the ground, and then took off leaving Jian and the other competition in the mud.

"Time to find my opponents," Pierce focused, floating south as fast as he could toward the castle wall. "Doug," he whispered. Nothing. "Doug," he whispered a little louder.

He heard rustling through the grass. Pierce turned around to look at the tree behind him but didn't see anything. Without moving he caught a shadow to his right out of his peripheral vision. He waited a moment, and then took off toward the perimeter of the wall. Pierce didn't know he could run as fast as his feet were moving.

"Look out," a voice yelled. Pierce jumped into the tall grass, and found his teammate.

"Where were you?" Pierce yelled to Doug in a loud whisper.

"I was sort of being followed," Doug answered.

"How's Skip?" Pierce asked.

"She's fine, I just left her," Doug said.

Two legs walked past slowly. Doug and Pierce crouched lower in the grass.

"We have to stick together," Doug suggested in a whisper.

"Yeah, I noticed other teams are splitting up," Pierce said. "I think that's a mistake though," he continued.

"Let's go toward the pond," Doug recommended.

"Why's that?" Pierce asked as they began to move slowly toward the pond.

"I have a feeling the gem is that way," Doug answered. "There," he said quickly.

"Where," Pierce asked.

"There," Doug pointed toward a boy in blue stripes running to a tree.

Pierce took off quietly and grabbed the boy before he knew what hit him. As Pierce tagged him, the boy's shirt began to glow. Suddenly the boy disappeared, and although Pierce didn't know where the boy disappeared to, he ended up in Skip's confinement.

"That is so much cooler than the flags we use at home," Pierce said to himself, wanting to make more opponents glow.

"One point for the newcomers," Eisenhut said to himself with a smile.

Although he wasn't in the general location of Doug and Pierce, he knew what was going on all over the vast field. Looking up, he wished his gift would make the rain go away. Then he had a second thought.

"They need to be prepared for whatever weather Ludicrous throws their way."

Scattered all over the field stood acre-wide clumps of trees. Given the size of the field in use during the competition, there were at least twenty acres of trees, which was going to make it difficult to find the gem. Skip stood by one of acre-clumps of trees. Suddenly, behind her, a boy in blue stripes appeared in the boundaries of her prison.

"This is so weird," she thought to herself.

"Another one," Pierce said, pointing toward a girl in a green polka dotted shirt.

Pierce snuck up behind and tagged her. Once again her shirt began to glow, and within an instant she disappeared. Skip saw the girl in green reappear in confinement a few moments later.

"Alright guys," she said cheering for Pierce and Doug from far away.

As the game went on, teams were being tagged one by one. Hunters were breaking their teammates free from jails, but Skip stayed strong, and no one could penetrate her area. She was able to tag a few as they came sneaking by her confinement.

After about an hour, Skip turned around as another one was beaming in, noticing it was Mae wearing, her team's red shirt. Ngai was the guard and Mae was now in their possession. Skip felt a twinge of anxiety thinking that Jian would try to break Mae free. After all, she was his sister.

Feeling a deep sense of awareness of her surroundings, Skip stood with cat-like balance. She heard woodland creatures scurry by, and then a branch break, and then silence. Feeling as though she had a sixth sense, she turned quickly toward a tree about twenty feet away. Lunging forward at the cause of the noise, she tagged a red shirted boy who began to have a deep reddish glow. Appearing behind her in jail was Jian, with a very disappointed look on his face. He knew that his team's two-year streak had ended.

"We need to go toward Skip," Doug whispered as they hid low to the ground.

"I got Jian," was all Doug heard in his head, inner voices taking over.

"Skip tagged Jian," Doug whispered to Pierce.

"How do you know?…Oh," Pierce answered his own question.

"Ahh," a voice yelled, as the person making it jumped toward Pierce.

Pierce jumped to the right and Doug to the left, and the boy fell to the ground.

"Get him," Doug yelled, knowing he was the prey not the predator and he couldn't tag anyone.

Pierce jumped and caught the boy's right sneaker, and his purple shirt began to glow. It was a guard that left his post. Doug and Pierce stood up and high fived each other in the imposing grass.

"Good call," Pierce said to Doug who remembered the rules.

"You're the speed, I'm the brains," Doug said with a smile. Then realizing that he may have hurt Pierce's feelings, he corrected himself.

"Let's face it. We're both the brains and the speed," Doug said. Pierce smiled.

"Ten minutes remaining," Eisenhut's voice boomed across the wooded field.

"How does he do that?" Doug asked.

"He's gifted," Pierce answered back quite seriously.

The boys were finally on their way toward Toaster Pond, but made a stop at their safety spot with Skip.

"Are you sure we can't get tagged here," Pierce asked the two of them.

"No, our jail is our safety," Skip answered.

Pierce turned and gave a friendly smile to Jian, who in return did not smile.

"How do we find a gem in all of this land," Pierce asked.

"Wait. Remember his rhyme," Skip asked. Rhymes and spells were beginning to become her strong suit.

"No," Pierce answered. Doug looked as though he was trying his best to remember the rhyme but couldn't.

Skip thought for a moment.

"You may look and look, and look you'll do. But find it where they're standing two," she repeated Eisenhut's rhyme.

"Standing too, what? He never finished the rhyme," Pierce said. Doug rolled his eyes.

"Not standing too but standing two," Doug said holding up two fingers. "We have to find those two refs from our game in Waterville," he explained. "The gem will be there. I don't know why I didn't think of it before."

"How do you know?" Pierce asked trying to be sure they were going in the right direction. "There are two huge trees that way, what if they're there?"

The rain was pouring down hard, and other teams were beginning to look exhausted. Doug, Skip and Pierce had no idea that at the moment they had the most captures. However, they were only winning by three.

"Look, there are teams all over there," Skip said pointing toward the two trees. "It's too obvious of a place. I say we go with Doug's idea."

"I can't get the two refs out of my mind. Parker is really important in this competition, and Gail is too. And they were both in Waterville. There are two of them, so I think we need to search them out," Doug said.

"Hurry, we don't have much time," Skip said anxiously agreeing with her cousin.

Doug and Pierce took off toward the center stage where Eisenhut was standing under an enormous maroon umbrella.

"Where did we see them last?" Pierce said.

"I didn't see them," Doug answered.

They made their way toward the stage. Eisenhut looked down with a smile. His goatee was just short enough that they saw a dimple on his right cheek.

"There," Pierce said pointing toward the two refs. Parker was standing looking solemn, and Gail was not breaking a smile either.

They reminded Doug of the guards at Buckingham Palace.

Doug ran over toward the referees and saw nothing on the ground. It was covered with mud and wet grass, but no gem. Parker and Gail stood statue like, not moving a muscle. It sort of freaked Doug out. He stopped and thought for a moment. Pierce stood still.

"You may look and look, and look you'll do. But find it where they're standing two." Doug looked up at Parker and there was a small green sparkle around his neck. He lunged and grabbed it off him. What looked like a rock began to gleam like a diamond.

"Whoa," Parker yelled, a little stunned by how aggressive Doug was.

The gleam of the gem was amazing, and it turned into a bright light shining toward the dark sky. The rain poured down but didn't seem to touch the gem.

"The gem has been found," Eisenhut announced with a smile.

"The game has ended," he commanded with a triple clap of his hands.

Doug and Pierce gave each other a high five, smiling from ear to ear. Every competitor stopped, as if overtaken by exhaustion.

"Congratulations," Gail Naylor said. It was the first time she spoke. "I knew you three had talent, but to get the most captures and the gem. That's not an easy thing to do."

Pierce and Doug stared at her, and Skip came running up with a smile.

"I'm sorry. I'm professor Gail Virginia Naylor. Congratulations," she said politely.

Skip, Doug and Pierce all smiled and said hello, feeling totally excited about their biggest win to date.

"Well, you three certainly have proven yourself worthy," Lord Eisenhut said congratulating the three competitors.

He leaned toward them, extending a congratulatory hand shake, and whispered, "I had no worries. I knew you would be the victors."

There had been a lot of pressure put on the three young competitors, and they never could have truly grasped how much pressure there was, but they came through.

"Thank you, Sir," they answered.

"Your dorm rooms will offer you sanctuary and a restful nap. You must be tired, and you're certainly wet," he said in a fatherly manner. "Tonight, after you clean up and rest, there will be a celebration," he said. Then he paused. "One thing though. How did you know where to find the gem?" he asked.

Skip smiled. "You may look and look, and look you'll do. But find it where they're standing two," she said.

We put it all together when we met at our post," she said, smiling toward Doug.

"Ah hah," he said, satisfied.

"Not only did you truly work as a team but you listened to my every word," he said. "Very important to do. Team work and direction following seem to be something of the past. You three seem to be re-instituting that," he confided. "There is always more than one way to look at a problem. Difficult problems are the most worthwhile to solve," he said with a grin. His dimples appeared over his goatee. "Let us go back to the castle and rest before tonight's celebration," he announced to everyone.

The crowd turned toward the Castle, and made their way back to their haven. The same lone crow quickly flew away toward Shadow Forest, and Lord Eisenhut knew exactly where she was flying.

As the new winners made their way through the crowd, they bumped into Jian and his teammates.

"Good Job," he simply said with a grin, and walked away.

Mae turned and gave a smile toward the team, as if she was relieved that she didn't have to enter Shadow Forest for the third year in a row, which made the three new winners a little less excited about their win.

Feeling wet, exhausted, anxious, and excited about the competition, they made their way up to their room.

"Insluipen," Doug said to the door, and it magically opened. The three plopped down on the floor in front of the warm lit fireplace that was waiting for them. Knowing they had a few hours before dinner, they wanted to rest. Their young bones and muscles were exhausted.

Sanger Castle was magical, and they were sure that they were in for the best celebration that they have ever seen.

Chapter 4.1
New Champions

D oug, Skip and Pierce were done cleaning up and felt refreshed after their long nap following the competition. Skip made her way out to the common room.

"Guys come here," she yelled.

Pierce and Doug ran into the room to see what Skip was yelling about. There was a colorful bouquet of flowers waiting for them.

"When did they get here?" Skip said, looking at her two friends as if they would know the answer.

"Must be when we were sleeping," Doug said, which sort of frightened him to think someone was in their suite when they were sleeping.

"There's a note," Pierce said, seeing a little white card on top of the flowers. Skip read it to her fellow victors.

> **Skip, Doug, and Pierce**
> **Congratulations on the win!**
> **The hardest part lies ahead.**
> **Enjoy this evening.**
> **We'll see you there!**
> **Dad and Gram**
>
> **p.s. Go back into your rooms and see**
> **what we left for you.**

The three smiled at the card, although separately they thought about the part that said,

"The hardest part lies ahead."

"Let's go see what they left for us," Skip yelled excitedly.

She came back out of her room wearing a long maroon ceremonial robe with soft black triangles all over it. Which contrasted perfectly with Doug's black robe with soft maroon triangles. Pierce walked out wearing a black robe identical to Doug's.

"Why are you wearing maroon?" Pierce asked Skip.

"It was the color left for me. Perhaps girls wear a different color for celebrations," she said.

Pierce grabbed the large brass doorknob to open the door, and they walked out of their room in anticipation of what lay ahead of them in the dining hall. There were two other dormitories besides Exodus that made up the castle sleeping areas, and the residents were all making their way to dinner as well.

"This place will be an awesome school when we get the Gem of Gicalma," Doug said to Skip and Pierce on the way down the spiral staircase.

All three realized that their mission was not over, and that their success or failure would determine if Sanger Castle became a school for the gifted, or a home for dark magic.

They were among many children who were walking to the dining hall, all wishing that they would be attending school at the castle in the fall.

Of course, today, Doug, Skip, and Pierce were three of the most popular children. Other children from the competition who were most likely captured by Pierce and guarded by Skip, were walking among then without hurt feelings. Even if they weren't on the same three-person team, they were a part of the team that represented the castle. Those teenagers who were gifted all needed to stick together. The world seemed unforgiving to those who were different.

As Skip, Doug, and Pierce made their way down the carpeted steps in their robes and padded clogs, they noticed a new picture in the hallway on the Wall of Fame. There was a picture of Doug, Skip, and Pierce together with Victory medals around their necks, standing in the dining hall on stage with Lord Eisenhut.

Ironically enough, the picture was never taken. Unless of course, that happened when they were sleeping as well.

The three looked at each other in amazement because they all realized at the same time that they never got their pictures taken after they won the Hide-and-Seek Competition. They also had never received a medal for winning. Skip had a slight smile as she realized that the pictures either show the past, or they look forward to the future.

"This is so cool," Doug said in a loud whisper to his friends.

Pierce and Skip smiled in agreement. Dr. Butterworth waited outside the dining hall for his son and two friends.

"Hello," he said with his deep voice and a smile.

Doug brushed his sandy brown hair out of his eyes as they all said hello in return. Dr. Butterworth grabbed Pierce and gave him a celebratory hug. Pierce felt proud at that moment.

"There you are. We were beginning to think you were going to nap through dinner," Corbin Gram, said as she made her way to meet up with the group.

"No way that was going to happen," Pierce said sarcastically referring to Sebastian, the very loud alarm clock. Dr. Butterworth smiled a bit.

"What's that smile for?" Pierce asked his father.

"Sebastian was my alarm clock when I first came here during the summers as a kid," he answered with a smile.

"That's an old alarm clock," Skip said out loud, and then wished she had said it to herself.

"Watch yourself, Skip," Dr. Butterworth said smiling.

"I don't suppose you want him back," Pierce asked interrupting.

"No thanks. He's there to keep you in line," his father replied.

"We have to go around back," Corbin Gram said interrupting the banter.

"Why?" Skip asked.

"The winners of the competition have to be announced and led into the dining hall a special way. It's tradition," Corbin Gram answered.

Doug, Pierce and Skip all felt quite special at the thought of being announced.

"Talk about making an entrance," Doug said to himself.

Corbin Gram then did something quite out of the ordinary. She made her way down to a life-sized portrait of Lord Eisenhut on the right side of the hallway, and simply asked to be allowed in.

"Won't you please let me enter," she said politely.

And with that, the portrait disappeared and Corbin Gram led the rest of the group through a hallway that was lit with torches.

"You didn't speak Latin," Doug said.

"Nor did I speak Dutch. You don't always have to speak a different language to get what you want. Sometimes simple manners are enough," Corbin Gram said with a smile.

"Besides, it works with the sound of your voice. It has an auditory spell, which means any unknown voice won't be allowed in," she explained.

There was a plush maroon carpet that flowed through the hall, and the three kids noticed a doorway ahead on their right. As they walked toward the doorway, all three kids found themselves quite nervous about the introduction they were about to receive.

In the waiting room the carpet was the same as the hallway and the room had a fireplace, which was lit, but the heat coming from it was not overwhelming. It seemed to be more for ambiance than warmth. All three of the competitors were happy that they got rid of the dampness they felt from the rainy Castle Cup, and they were feeling famished.

"Welcome to our waiting room," Lord Eisenhut said entering the room from a completely different doorway. "Usually only the professors and Barons are allowed in here, but we make allowances once a year for our champions."

Pierce tried hard not to beam with pride at being called a champion. Skip and Doug relished the thought a bit, too.

"Where do all of these hallways go?" Doug asked.

"Ahhh, Doug. You're always curious. That's wonderful," Eisenhut answered showing his right dimple above his thick goatee. "There are many secret passageways through this castle.

Most castles have hundreds of secret corridors," Eisenhut explained. "It was, and is, a way for people to escape if any unforeseen circumstances occur," he confided.

Pierce, Skip and Doug got a slight chill from the thought of unforeseen circumstances.

"However, you must be careful in a castle too. There are a few frightening rooms around here. We actually have one we believe is haunted. No matter how much heat we throw in, it never warms up. And there are some others, but-perhaps another time. Just be careful around here," Eisenhut said as if he were warning the three newcomers.

Eisenhut also realized that he sparked the curiosity of the three new champions, which is exactly what he wanted to do.

"Shall we enter soon, Sir?" Dr. Butterworth asked.

"Duncan, are you feeling hungry?" Eisenhut said with a grin.

Pierce's Dad shook his head with a polite no. Dr. Butterworth was more concerned that his son and two friends didn't go wandering about in a castle that was mostly friendly, but not forgiving.

"I am," Pierce interjected.

The adults laughed, knowing that all three children had voracious appetites.

"Tonight will be slightly different than normal," Lord Eisenhut began.

"Normal," Doug thought. "This place is far from normal."

Skip smiled as if she knew what Doug was thinking.

"Let me explain what will happen," Eisenhut said. "I will enter the dining hall with Dr. Butterworth and Professor Corbin, where all of your peers are eating hors d'oeuvres. I will give a clap of my hands, and then introduce you. A few horns may blow as well," Eisenhut whispered jokingly.

Doug noticed how proud his grandmother was to be called a professor. He had a strong desire to walk in her footsteps.

"Ahh. It seems to be time," Lord Eisenhut, said as if someone came and whispered in his ear.

"I'm proud of all of you," Dr. Butterworth said, as he followed

Eisenhut out toward the stage.

"Your parents are very proud as well," Corbin Gram said, making her entrance into the dining hall.

"You mean they know?" Skip said.

"Of course they know. Who else would they want to break their record of four wins," Corbin Gram said with a grin.

"This has been the weirdest two days," Doug said.

"But the best," Pierce answered back.

"Clap...clap...clap," Lord Eisenhut's big hands collided together making noise much louder than the eating and conversing that was taking place around the dining hall. Everyone stopped what they were doing, and he had their full attention.

"I would like to welcome all of you to this joyful occasion. Everyone played brilliantly today," he said, offering up his congratulations.

"However, only one team could be the victors. And they did so, by not only capturing the most teams, but also the Castle gem." The facial expressions among the crowd ranged from being happy, to envious, to disappointed. "We would like to welcome our new champions of this year's Castle Cup Hide-and-Seek competition. They are Skip Corbin, Douglas Manion, and Pierce Butterworth," he announced clapping wildly.

The rest of the dining hall erupted in applause, realizing that they were there for one common goal, which was to get the real gem from Shadow Forest and Ludicrous Zwevil. The precious Gem of Gicalma.

With the sound of the crowd applauding, Skip, Doug and Pierce walked slowly out to the stage where all of the Barons and Professors were standing with Lord Eisenhut. They were amazed by what they saw when looking out toward the crowd.

The dining tables were set up in three, one hundred foot long tables. The tables were covered with maroon tablecloths that went down the middle length-wise, leaving the wood exposed where each teenager would be sitting.

It looked as though a King and his soldiers were going to be sitting at the medieval style settings at any moment. Hanging from the ceiling were nine large chandeliers that were filled with lit candles.

There was no need for servants because the meals appeared, and then disappeared when everyone finished their first course.

Doug, Skip, and Pierce were all awarded gold medals that hung on hunter green neck piece matching their uniforms from the competition. The three could not help but notice how much their stance and medals looked like the one from the picture hanging on the Wall of Fame. At once, a flash lit up the room, nearly blinding the three champions. It was as if someone was taking their picture. However, no one was standing with a camera.

"Please sit with us at our head table and enjoy your dinner," Eisenhut offered to them.

At the same moment, the lights flickered a bit, and Eisenhut had a look of worry on his face. He glanced over at the Barons and Professors, and Dr. Butterworth offered a nod in his direction, understanding the conversation that would soon take place. Everyone in the dining hall moaned with worry.

"No time for resting on your laurels," he said to the three champions.

Pierce was unclear about Eisenhut's meaning, but Doug and Skip understood.

"Now, now," Eisenhut said loudly to dull the roar of the nervous crowd. "We have the best competitors we have had in twenty or more years. I have no doubt that things will return to normal. Or even get better in the next few days," he said half talking to the endless crowd of boys and girls, and half sending a polite warning to the three champions.

Doug could feel himself become anxious. Skip found herself nervous, but wouldn't let on. Pierce was psyched for the challenge.

After the frozen moment of the light flickering, they made their way back to their dinner places, and sat down to eat, feeling famished from the competition. They knew they had to eat enough to keep up their strength for their future challenge.

"Slow down Manion. No one is going to take it away from you," Skip remarked to Doug as he began eating.

He was a little embarrassed by how fast he was eating, and looked around to see if anyone else besides his cousin was watching him shovel food down like it was going out of style. Luckily he was in the clear because everyone else was too busy talking or eating.

Except for his grandmother, who caught his eye and mouthed the words, "SLOW DOWN" to him as she smiled at her hungry young grandson.

He felt his face turn as red as Skip's hair. Growing up on a farm made him appreciate food. It kept him strong and energetic to feed and milk the cows and bale hay. He needed his energy more than ever now. Actually, he was hoping for a day's rest before he had to go into Shadow Forest.

As the invisible waiters and waitresses were taking their main plate away, the south wall expanded and the castle orchestra appeared. Doug had assumed it was the castle orchestra, because he couldn't imagine another orchestra being on tour in Sangerfield.

"They're quite good," Lord Eisenhut bragged, mostly to himself, but also to whoever was listening.

He walked over to tell the three kids from Waterville about the orchestra. Pierce was never very impressed by classical music. Skip didn't have a strong opinion for it or against it, but Doug loved it.

"Mr. Culture is in his glory," Pierce said jokingly about Doug.

"Yes, well, it's mostly made up of professors that will stay for the upcoming school year...depending on...well, you already know," Lord Eisenhut said, and floated back to his table place so he could listen properly. All three kids almost lost their appetite knowing it was all up to them.

They hadn't been at the castle for more than a couple of days, but were getting used to their surroundings and liked being there. The rekindling with a grandmother they thought they lost, and truly finding out where Pierce's dad had disappeared to was the best experience they ever had. Being the only ones to capture the gem was a lot of pressure for the three thirteen year olds, but it was a challenge they mostly welcomed. After all, they came from a long line of excellent Hide-and-Seekers from the small town of Waterville. A very magical town.

"This music seems to last forever," Pierce grumbled, as everyone else seemed to be smiling at the sound of the orchestra.

"It's actually only one part of it," Doug said back to him.

"You're kidding. There's more?" Pierce asked in disappointed amazement.

"Yeah, this is called Summer from Vivaldi. There are three more pieces to it," Doug said proudly, but almost pompously.

"Let me guess," Pierce said sourly.

"Spring, Fall and Winter are the other pieces," he said.

"Way to go Einstein," Skip said with a smile.

Another boy turned around to look at them. They realized it was the same look you get when you're talking during a movie, so they stopped and listened.

After another few minutes of musical pleasure for Doug and Skip, and musical pain for Pierce, the orchestra stopped. Eisenhut stood up and clapped wildly. The rest of the dining hall stood as well, and gave the Sanger Castle Orchestra a standing ovation. Suddenly the orchestra disappeared back behind the large brick wall that reappeared.

"Final course, please," Lord Eisenhut announced, and suddenly cheesecake, crème faiche, orange sorbet, and a whole list of other desserts appeared in front of every child.

"It's like they can read our minds and know what dessert we like," Skip said in amazement.

"Well that's not too hard for me," Doug jumped in, "I like everything," he said laughing.

All of the children in the dining hall spent the better part of five minutes eating their dessert with very little conversation. Doug felt full, as did most of the children.

"They certainly know how to feed us," Doug commented.

Looking around at the way the other children were sitting, Doug could tell he wasn't the only one who thought so. Boys and girls were leaning back, trying to relax after they indulged the extremely filling meals. Although the food was great, Doug, Skip, and Pierce had more on their minds, and exploring the castle was their number one priority.

Chapter 4.2
A Small Adventure

As all the young diners dispersed from the dining hall toward the dormitories, Doug, Skip, and Pierce went in the opposite direction wanting to explore the castle a little more. Doug carefully looked around to make sure they weren't being watched. Wandering in the direction of Eisenhut's living quarters, they made their way down a long empty corridor. It was completely dark.

"Can you see anything?" Skip asked.

"No, what about you?" Doug answered.

"Not a thing," Skip answered in return.

"Pierce…" they said at the same time. "Pierce," nothing.

"Where's Pierce?" Skip asked Doug.

At that moment they heard the flick of a match and turned around.

"Hey guys," Pierce said with a smile on his face and a brightly lit torch in his hand.

"Where'd you get that?" Skip asked.

"The torch was on the wall and the matches were in my robe pocket," he said.

"Where'd you get matches?" Skip asked.

"I just told you…oh, you mean where did I get them originally?" he asked. Skip gave him a look, and he instantly knew the answer.

"I'm not sure. They just appeared," Pierce answered.

Walking through the semi-lit hallway, they saw portraits of unknown people on the walls. Unlike the photos from the Wall of Fame, these were painted portraits. They were of both men and women. Some of them looked rather old, but none of them were familiar to Doug, Skip and Pierce.

"Where do you want to go?" Pierce asked.

At that same moment they heard a noise down the hall. There was a banging noise, and then a voice. Bang again, and then the same voice.

"What's going on?" Skip said to Doug, hoping her cousin's inner voices were working.

"I have no idea," Doug answered.

"What about your voices?" she asked again, feeling a bit impatient.

"Not working," Doug said simply.

They walked closer and closer, not knowing what they would see. As they got closer, only one voice was heard, and it was a female who seemed to be talking to herself. The door to the room was closed, so they kept the torch lit. Pierce stood with his ear to the door, and Skip kneeled below him doing the same thing. Doug stood back holding the torch that Pierce handed him.

"What's going on?" Doug whispered.

"Shhh, I can't hear anything," Skip whispered back.

"Tonight, tonight, the beasts come out.
They jump around, and scream and shout.
Run away, before they see.
They're after you. They're after me.
I am afraid, I am in fear.
Allow me now, to disappear,"
And then there was nothing.

"Bang," it sounded like someone fell to the floor. "No, that didn't work," the voice said again. It sounded like another English woman, like Baroness Choukeir, only the accent was slightly different.

"We should go," Doug whispered feeling nervous by the surroundings. Skip and Pierce agreed, and turned around and began to make their way back.

"Excuse muy," the voice said from behind them. The three turned around slowly, scared of what they might see and nervous that trouble was coming their way.

Standing in front of them was a woman in a black robe with flaming red hair and dark black-rimmed cat-eye glasses. She stood a bit shorter than Doug and Skip, and had the oddest-looking purple earrings, which perfectly matched her purple shoes.

"Ello," she said in her heavy accent. "You Blokes are the new ones aren't ya," she asked, already knowing the answer.

"Yes, Ma'am, Pierce answered.

"Dr. Butterworth's son, Professor Corbin's grandchildren heh," she said, although they weren't sure if she was asking them a question. "Don't look so nervous dearies," she said to the three. "Ya think you'll be getting inta trouble do ya?" she said.

Skip and Doug nodded in agreement with her question. Considering they were wandering around the castle after hours. Or at least they thought it was after hours. All they knew is that they snuck out in the opposite direction from everyone else.

"Well now. You won't be gettin into trubble with me. It's not curfew yet," she assured them.

"Are you from England, too?" Skip asked.

"No, no dear. I'm frum Ireland," she said. "Land of tha wee lil' people," she said holding her hand close to the floor referring to leprechauns.

"Really," Pierce said with his mouth gaping open.

"No, me dear. I'm just joshen ya," she said laughing. "How rude of me. I'm Professor Fahlzalot. Tripolina Fahlzalot actually," she introduced herself with a grin.

"There is no way that can be her real name," Doug thought to himself.

"Come into my room, won't ya?" she asked, and as she turned to walk into the room, hit the wall and fell.

"Ma'am are you alright?" the three said running to help her up.

Doug realized that if Tripolina Fahlzalot was her real name, it was certainly fitting.

"Oh yes. I do that sort of thin all tha time. Won't ya come in?" she asked, walking safely into her room after the second attempt at trying to enter.

The room looked like it was part classroom and part laboratory. Calling it colorful would be an understatement. It had rainbows painted toward the ceiling and trees and a tree cabin painted on the back wall. It seemed that Professor Fahlzalot had a love for poetry, because there were poems written on all the walls in permanent marker of a variety of colors. There were lights with light bulbs, not candles hanging from the ceiling. There was a wooden workbench, but also three long wooden tables in the middle of the room. They were much like the tables in the dining hall, but only about a quarter of the length. On the walls beside the murals were portraits, only these were of people Doug recognized, like Einstein, Robert Frost, and Beethoven, along with women and men he didn't recognize.

"Do you like me room?" she said with a proud smile.

The three onlookers simply nodded their heads feeling a bit overwhelmed by the art. The one thing they could tell was that Tripolina Fahlzalot was not only the most flamboyant person they had ever met, but also one of the happiest.

Doug looked over at the portraits with a questioning gaze.

"Professor Fahlzalot, may we ask you a something?" Doug began.

"Yes, me dear. What is it?" she asked politely.

"Were Einstein and Beethoven professors here?" he asked.

Fahlzalot began laughing hysterically. She didn't seem to care whether it hurt Doug's feelings or not.

"Why, Heavens, no. I'm just a huge fan of their work," she said.

Doug was a bit embarrassed that he asked the question. Skip and Pierce both stood motionless, feeling relieved that they hadn't asked. Although they didn't see what was so funny about it.

"What is it you do here?" Skip asked, just as she did with Baron Doha.

"Do?" Fahlzalot began. "I teach. I educate, I instruct," she said slowly enunciating her words.

Fahlzalot began to walk toward the enormous chalkboard, then tripped and fell on her face banging her nose against the floor, which much to the surprise of the onlookers, didn't bleed, nor did it knock off her thick black eyeglasses. Doug, Skip, and Pierce all ran to assist her, but by the time they got to her, she was standing again.

"I am so sorry. It's quite all right. You see, I seem to…to," she stuttered as if she couldn't find the right words.

"Fall a lot," Skip said for her.

"Yes, me dear. I certainly du," she answered as if she saw no correlation between her name and her inability to walk. "I simply don't know what's wrong with me. I just stumble, trip,…I fall a lot," she said laughing in a flamboyantly strange way.

Doug, Pierce, and Skip were somewhat taken aback by Professor Fahlzalot, but they were beginning to like her a great deal. She was unbelievably clumsy, but extremely sincere in her efforts to make the newcomers feel welcome in their new surroundings.

"So why is it you three seem to be sneaking around e're anyway?" she asked politely with her Irish accent.

"Uhm..uhhmm." Skip began stuttering.

"Out with it now laddies," Fahlzalot said with a more serious tone.

"We couldn't help ourselves," Doug confided not being able to think up a better answer.

"Well, now. Aren't you an honest bloke," she said in return. "I have somethin for ya. Although I didn't realize it would be yours until now," she said walking over to her extremely messy desk.

Surprisingly enough, she didn't trip once on the way to her destination. However, on the way back was a different matter. She walked and caught her purple shoe on a chair, and slid a good five yards right to Doug's feet.

"Oh yes, now then," was all she could say looking at the expressions of the three teenagers as she lifted herself from the ground. "You see me dearies, I teach about herbs. And I heard you may be having a love for that," she said referring to Skip.

"Yes," Skip replied.

She handed Skip a small pouch with several sample bottles in it. "What is this for?" Skip asked looking inside.

Professor Fahlzalot took out one small bottle with cream inside, holding it up so the three could see it. "This is *Aloe*. It offers you protection and luck," she said putting it back in, and grabbed another bottle with the word *Basil* on it.

"Isn't that for cooking?" Pierce asked.

"Ahh, me Laddie. Basal isn't just for cooking anymore," Fahlzalot answered. "A little Basil can help ya fly," she said with a smile, and then put it away before they could ask her another question. Once she put the bottle back in, she grabbed another one labeled *Dandelion*.

"This one lets ya call onta spirits to help ya when ya are in need," she said, and then grabbed another bottle labeled *Bergamot*. "This is somethin ya can uz on a weak-minded enemy in tha forest. It iz called Bergamot, and it will help ya change thar mood from dangerous, ta cheerful. Remember though Laddies," she said lowering her voice to a soft whisper. "I said weak minded."

Handing Doug a notepad she went through many other herbs and explained them. Fahlzalot began with *Cedar wood* and went to *Chamomile*. She grabbed several more small bottles labeled *Cyprus* and *Jasmine*.

"How big is that bag?" Skip asked, noticing how many bottles were being pulled out of such a small pouch.

"It's deep enough," Fahlzalot answered. "You need to use that wisely," Fahlzalot began. "You will need them when you enter Shadow Forest. Along with yur necklace dearie," she said looking at Doug.

Doug wasn't sure how Fahlzalot knew about the magical necklace, but he didn't question anything in Sanger Castle.

"When you're invisible you will leave footprints, so be very careful," she warned, and began to tidy up her untidy room. "Now. I need ya ta go back to your suite....quickly will ya... Ya need all the information ya can get before ya go, and I gave ya a little. Tomorrow will be a big day. Yes, a big day for ya all,"

Fahlzalot said. "I don't think ya should be hanging around much longer here, don't you know," she said repeating herself with different words. "Make your way back to your suite. Use the necklace, if you need, for practice. And good luck to ya laddies. Be gifted and be true. Be yourself...be you," she said wisely, and then suddenly, she disappeared.

The whole conversation seemed to be a haze in their minds. She was odd, but probably the most favorite character they had met at Sanger Castle. Excluding Dr. Butterworth and Corbin Gram, of course.

"This is going to be so wild," Pierce said feeling dazed.

"Let's get going back," Skip said.

Doug played with the necklace around his neck, and grabbed the hands of his two friends. He looked at them and closed his eyes to focus on disappearing. And with that, the friends vanished, and made their way safely back down the very quiet and empty hallway, up the spiral staircase, and toward their suite.

"Insluipen," Pierce said, and the doors opened.

They found themselves tired from the long day. Any other time in their lives they would have loved to stay up past ten, but couldn't muster the energy this evening. All three brushed their teeth, got ready for bed within minutes, and were out cold by nine. They were exhausted from the day, but anxious for the events that lay ahead of them.

Chapter 4.3
Gifts

T he next morning, Doug and Pierce woke up before the sound of their alarms, much to Pierce's pleasure. Pierce was quite happy he didn't have to put up with Sebastian's abuse. Although secretly, he enjoyed the back and forth banter that they had been sharing for the past two days.

Two days… Pierce could not believe everything that had taken place in the past two days. Given that he had prior knowledge of Sanger Castle before he arrived, he thought he would be prepared for everything he and his best friends experienced. However, it was more than his imagination could have mustered up, and it was going to take some time to get used to not seeing his mother as often as before. He did feel fortunate to have his dad around, though.

The boys heard Skip walking around the living area of the suite and went out to meet her before they went to breakfast in the dining hall. It was fun for them to spend so much time together, and knowing that their parents knew their whereabouts; they felt a little more relaxed about being away for so long.

"Good morning," they all said in monotone voices to each other.

None of them were morning people, and sounded as if they were adults who were in need of their first cup of percolated coffee.

"We should head down to breakfast and then go and see Eisenhut," Doug suggested.

"I'm sure he'll find us before we find him," Skip chimed in.

Although they just woke up, anxiety about Shadow Forest was setting in, and they wanted to learn as much as possible about their adventure before setting off to enter into the land of trees.

"What do you think the other gifts are going to be?" Pierce asked, as they walked out the door.

"Who knows? I never would have thought that we would have a necklace of invisibility," Doug answered.

It all seemed like a dream to them. However, it was very real, and tomorrow was going to be a dose of unimaginable reality. They all could agree upon that.

The three champions walked into the crowded dining hall, grabbed trays, and stood in line to get breakfast.

"Good morning," a slight English voice said from behind.

It was Valeo, and she had an important message.

"Lord Eisenhut would like you to meet him in his study after breakfast," she said.

They were hoping they would remember how to get to Eisenhut's study. After devouring breakfast, they walked out the exit toward the right. The hallway seemed to stretch for a mile, and they found themselves alone in a hallway lit with candles. Candles were not as helpful as real lights, but choices were limited.

"Conserving energy," Skip said.

"That's why we're here," Pierce answered, focusing on the job at hand.

As Skip and Pierce were talking, Doug spotted the portrait of Lord Sanger, and he walked over to it.

"Ingressus," Doug said in Latin, and the portrait moved to the side. Eager to hear Eisenhut's words of wisdom, they quickly walked through the corridor to the doors that led into his study.

"Unity," Doug said as he looked at the symbolic doorknobs. Skip and Pierce nodded in agreement, feeling very unified.

Doug politely knocked on the huge solid wood doors. Although he meant for it to be a soft knock, it echoed through the hallway.

The doors slowly opened, but no one was on the other side pulling them open. When all three walked in, Eisenhut was sitting behind an enormous mahogany desk.

"Good morning. I have been expecting you," he said to the three as if he knew they were coming at that moment.

The three teenagers returned the greeting.

"Sit down, please," he said. "We have a lot to talk about."

"How did you know we were coming?" Pierce asked.

"It's called an intercom, and someone called to tell me you were coming," he said with a smile. "Not everything belongs to the gift."

Eisenhut had a big smile knowing full well that it was a rather anticlimactic answer to Pierce's question. All four let out a nervous laugh, although Eisenhut's was loud, rather amusing himself.

"How did you sleep last night?" Lord Eisenhut asked like a concerned parent.

"Fine, good, great," they all said at the same time.

"Good, I'm glad," he said in return. "I know that you were given some information by Professor Fahlzalot," he began.

The three nodded in agreement.

"I would like to share the rest," he said slowly choosing his words.

"First of all. I want you to understand that your parents know exactly where you are," he said.

"We know, Corbin Gram told us," Doug answered.

Even though they knew, Doug felt relieved that his mother was supportive of his being at Sanger Castle.

"Your parents were contacted by my wife as soon as you made your way into the pond. They're very excited that you made it safely, and that you won the competition. (As if there was any concern there). You are from Waterville. We have a reputation to uphold," he said profoundly with a smile. "On to some more important information," he began.

Eisenhut paused, choosing every word carefully.

"Tomorrow will be extremely dangerous," he said.

"If that's his way of easing us into the situation, then he needs some work on his delivery," Doug thought.

"I don't want you to think this is going to be a game, because you could be killed. I'm not proud that we have to send in teenagers, but unfortunately, the spell controls that situation," he said seriously. "In the past, children have not come back, and were never accounted for," Eisenhut explained gravely. "And I'm not exactly on speaking terms with Ludicrous Zwevil, so I never could get information." This was the understatement of the century. "Their poor parents never got over losing their children," Eisenhut said sadly.

Doug thought he saw a tear form on the Lord's cheek, but didn't want to stare and make him uncomfortable. After a moment of silence, Eisenhut stood up, and waved a hand at the empty white wall in his room that stood next to his fireplace. The picture of an ugly troll came up on the wall.

"What's that?" Skip asked in disgust.

"It's a Forest Troll, and as repulsed as you are of it. It feels the same way about you. It will be looking for you tomorrow when you enter Shadow Forest," Eisenhut warned.

With the wave of his hand a second time, a picture of an animal that looked similar to the troll came up, making the troll look handsome. It was small, with big floppy ears, and a reddened face with warts. It also looked as if it drooled, and had fangs sticking up from its bottom jaw like a troll.

"This is a spriggan," said Eisenhut. "It stands four feet tall, like a troll, but when it gets angry, it inflates to twice that size," Eisenhut warned again. "These are just two creatures that you may have to battle. But use your wit, because a weapon is no match for it," Eisenhut cautioned.

Doug was hoping that he had his wits about him because the creatures were not the kind he wanted to run into in the forest.

"Besides, we don't use weapons. We like using our common sense.

Weapons are a last resort," he added.

"What do the other ones look like?" Skip asked.

"The third is this," and a picture of a giant came up on the wall.

Its hair was dirty and greasy. In addition, it had enormous teeth in a very large mouth, and was wearing a shirt that was too tight and pants that were too small.

"This is a giant," he simply explained.

Doug, Skip and Pierce could only think that giant was the perfect name for him, because he was just that....giant.

"I have a way to defeat this particular creature, but you need to bring this one back alive," Eisenhut said coyly. "His name is Khalil Flatbottom," Eisenhut said looking at the creature.

"That... this has a name?" Skip stuttered.

"We have to bring him back," Doug said calmly. Although on the inside he was screaming.

"Khalil didn't always look like that. He was...special," Eisenhut said with fondness. "As if getting the Gem of Gicalma isn't enough, we are sure you will run into Khalil. And we want you to use this when you do," he said.

The three waited to hear a special spell, or see some magic dust. Eisenhut reached into his robe and pulled out a small mirror. Doug, Skip and Pierce thought it was a joke. Eisenhut laughed, knowing what they were thinking.

"With all due respect, Sir," Pierce said. "What are we going to do with a mirror?"

"Ahh," Eisenhut began. "You," pointing to Skip, "will do much with it," he said confidently. "Can you imagine being as ugly as a troll, spriggan or giant, and seeing your reflection?" Eisenhut asked matter-of-factly, which was a good point. They couldn't imagine being that frightening looking and wanting to look in the mirror.

"Why me?" Skip said taking the mirror as Eisenhut handed it to her in a small velvet pouch. It was the second pouch she had to carry.

"Because you are the guard, and this will help you guard your teammates. Along with the herbs and the Book of Spells that is sitting in your suite, you will be well-equipped to handle these unfortunate creatures," he answered. "As soon as a troll, or a spriggan sees itself, it will melt," Eisenhut said. "It is the Mirror of Truth. A creature cannot stand to see it's true complexion, but a man hiding behind the face of a creature will turn back into its human form. Be careful with it, it is a powerful tool," Eisenhut warned.

He allowed time for his words to sink in for the three teenagers. It was quite a bit to comprehend, and Eisenhut knew they still wouldn't understand the magnitude of the situation until they faced one of the three creatures.

"We need to move on," Eisenhut said. "If you can get a gem, then we can begin our goal of opening the castle and making it a school. It's not something we could do before, because we didn't have the power, or the confidence. Things have changed since you three came," he said.

Doug, Skip, and Pierce looked confused.

"Why us?" Doug asked not feeling very confident or special.

"Because you are the three best players we have ever seen, and we're sending you to look for a gem that is the hardest to find. With that gem, our worries will be over for quite a long time," he began. "Ludicrous Zwevil guards this gem with her life. If you capture this gem, it would rid us of our spell that requires us to have a gem for energy as often as we do. With the Gem of Gicalma, we would not have to worry about acquiring another gem, ever," he confided. "A lot falls on your shoulders."

The three knew the gem would be helpful, but didn't realize it would be the last one needed. If they could just accomplish this one mission, then they would solidify the castle becoming a school for the gifted.

"When do you want us to leave?" Pierce asked.

Eisenhut smiled and said, "I like your eagerness. You are a lot like your father," he said.

Pierce loved the compliment.

"You need to leave within the next twenty four hours. But do it when you see fit," he said. "It is all up to you."

Pierce, Skip, and Doug stood up, filled with nervousness and anticipation.

"I will not see you until you return. Good luck and use the tools you have acquired," Eisenhut hinted. "There will be one more given before you go," he said. "Dr. Butterworth and Corbin Gram will be by to deliver it."

The three teenagers turned and walked toward the door. The

journey back to their suite was filled with silence. No one wanted to say a word about their conversation with Eisenhut.

Climbing the stairs, Skip began to feel anxious about her part in the mission. As the guard, a lot rested on her shoulders.

"When do you want to go?" Skip asked.

"Dusk," Doug and Pierce said together.

The fact that they answered together, cemented their thoughts that they knew the best time to leave.

"I thought we were going tomorrow?" Skip asked.

"I think we need to get a head start in case Eisenhut isn't the only one who knows when we're entering Shadow Forest," Doug suggested, referring to Ludicrous Zwevil.

One more gift and the adventure would begin. They sat in their suite, sitting in silence contemplating the adventure before them, and the many other adventures they already experienced.

"Knock, knock, knock," came the banging at the door.

"Who is it?" Skip asked,

"It's us," two familiar voices said behind her.

Corbin Gram and Dr. Butterworth were standing behind Skip; although a second earlier they were knocking at the door.

"How did…" Skip stopped, and thought out loud. "Why knock if you're going to appear behind me anyway?" she said perplexed.

"We wanted to give you some warning before we came in," Pierce's Dad answered.

Pierce, Skip and Doug were all really happy to see the familiar faces of Corbin Gram and Dr. Butterworth.

"We've come on Castle business," Corbin Gram said, getting to the point.

Skip, Doug, and Pierce were surprised by her serious tone.

"Let's have a seat," Dr. Butterworth suggested.

The three teenagers sat on the black leather couch and the adults stood in front of them.

"We have your final gift," the adults said together.

"Pierce, I believe this one belongs to you," his father said handing him a beaded necklace. It was filled with black, silver, and white beads in a pattern of three.

"What does it do?" Pierce asked carefully.

Corbin Gram and Dr. Butterworth noticed that the three kids were now used to the fact that the gifts given provided some sort of gift in return.

"It changes the train of thought for people," Corbin Gram said.

The three kids were a little confused.

"What do you mean?" asked Pierce.

His father spoke up. "If you wear this necklace, it will help persuade any enemies to agree with you. Just in case you get split up and are without the herbs."

Doug, Pierce, and Skip did not like the thought of being split up. It was actually a thought that never occurred to them. Realizing that they were without a plan, they gave their full attention to the two adults.

"For instance, if you meet up with a forest troll, and it is preventing you from getting by, strongly suggest to him that he should let you by, and he will do as you command," his father explained.

"You don't yell, or get physical. All you have to do is speak in an even tone and stare into his eyes," Butterworth continued, with a smile on his face. It was as if he had used the necklace many times. "It works on people with weak minds," his father added.

"Pierce, it is important that you are the only one to use it, and use it wisely. It is a powerful tool, but you three need to work together," Corbin Gram explained. Dr. Butterworth was nodding his head in agreement.

"Well, I guess this means we can leave soon," Doug said nervously.

"Not yet. There's more," Corbin Gram said.

Behind her the double doors to the suite opened by themselves, and there were three small backpacks, with some sort of insect flying above them.

"The bags have food in them, including water...when you need them.

Do not drink the water in the forest," Professor Butterworth warned.

Upon closer inspection, they all focused on the fact that it wasn't an insect flying above the bags, but a tiny girl with wings. "Is that an actual fairy?" asked Skip with disbelief.

With that question, the fairy flew in and introduced herself.

"Yeah, I'm a fairy," she said sarcastically.

Pierce couldn't help notice that the fairy had six toes.

"What r you looking at," she said looking directly at Pierce.

Pierce was stunned and didn't know how to answer her. He knew he was busted staring at her oddity, and his father snickered behind his son's back at the conflict that was arising.

It was bad enough he was looking at an actual fairy, but a six-toed fairy was a bit too much.

"Now, now. Don't be rude, introduce yourself," Corbin Gram said to the fairy.

"I'm Felicia," the fairy said flatly.

She saw the looks of amazement on the faces of the three teenagers.

"Yeah, that's right. I'm Felicia the six toed fairy," she said.

"Anyone have anything to say?" she said with quite an attitude.

"No, no…no," the three shocked teenagers said staring at the fairy.

"Where are you from?" Skip asked intrigued by the accent.

"Here," Felicia said quickly.

"Felicia. Be nice. You're here to help them out. And yourself, we might add," Butterworth said authoritatively.

Felicia's demeanor changed a bit at the lecture, and her accent was less thick, and more polite.

"Sorry," she apologized.

"Felicia will accompany you through the forest. No one knows it better than she," Corbin Gram chimed in to explain Felicia's nervousness.

At the same time, Dr. Butterworth handed the three new clothes for their mission. There were black pants, long sleeved shirts, black socks, and dark sneakers to match. Along with the dark clothes, they were handed cloaks as well.

"A little warm for the summer, don't you think?" Skip asked.

"The forest is cold during the day, as well as the night," Butterworth said.

"Besides, some of the bugs are not the kind by which you would want to be bitten," Corbin Gram explained.

Doug was not very excited about the idea of a new species of bug. After they had spent an hour together, Butterworth and Corbin Gram knew it was time to say goodbye.

"Good luck," Pierce's Dad said to them. "We're very proud of you three already. We know you can acquire the Gem of Gicalma," he said confidently.

"You come from a long line of Waterville Hide-and-Seekers, including your fathers and their parents before that," Corbin Gram began.

"You have all the tools you need. You are athletic, but most of all, you're gifted. That will help you more than you know."

All of the relatives embraced, and Corbin Gram and Pierce's Dad walked out the double doors.

"Well, when are we going?" Felicia asked abruptly.

"Soon," Doug answered.

"What's with the tone?" Felicia asked.

"I'll tell you when you tell me," Doug snapped.

"Guys, stop. We need to work together," Pierce chimed in.

"One last question?" Pierce said sitting in their living area.

"What?" Felicia answered.

"If you're an all powerful fairy, why the six toes?" he asked with a smile.

"Nice," she began. "I don't have a lot of power. I'm just small, Einstein. You'd know that if you'd read a little. And the six toes are genetic. Any more questions?" she asked.

"We'll be leaving in a few hours. It'll be dusk by then and we can slip out," Doug said interrupting them.

He was ready for the mission, but wasn't sure he was ready for what he was going to see when they got to the forest. None of them seemed ready for Felicia the six-toed fairy.

The thought of gnomes, forest elves, giants, and other

creatures that he couldn't even remember, had Doug a bit anxious. However, the most important job of his life lay ahead, and he planned on getting the Gem of Gicalma.

The idea of being famous twirled around in his head, although that wasn't the only reason he wanted to capture the gem. He loved his new-found surroundings, and liked the idea of the castle becoming a school for the gifted. It would be a nice change from the school he was presently attending. Not that Waterville Junior High wasn't nice, but Sanger Castle provided him the experience of being with kids that all wanted to be in school. It just seemed to be a little more dangerous than being in Waterville, but that added to the excitement of being here. He couldn't believe that his mother and father knew that he was here, and that they used to spend their summers at Sanger Castle, too.

Doug realized that his mother wasn't upset at the funeral because her mother had passed away, but she was upset with the fact that her mother moved away, and she knew that Doug was going to be leaving soon as well.

It was all beginning to make sense. He wondered how Beck was dealing with his disappearance, but figured his parents were taking care of that end of things. Secretly, he missed Beck and her annoying everyday habits. That was what a little sibling's job was, to annoy their older siblings. Doug didn't realize how much he enjoyed the banter back and forth until it wasn't there anymore.

Now it was his job and the job of his two teammates to make their families, …(and families they didn't even know), proud of them. They held the hopes of a castle, and all the inhabitants and future inhabitants in their hands. The three friends weren't about to let any of them down.

"Hey, what are you thinking about?" Pierce asked Doug as if he didn't already know the answer.

"Nothing, I'm just a bit nervous," Doug answered.

"We are too," Skip said behind them.

"You should be," Felicia said. "That place is dangerous. Many have entered Shadow Forest and never came out," she continued.

"I mean, there were kids who were..." Felicia began.

"We get the point. We've heard the story already," Pierce interrupted.

Felicia stopped, and actually looked like her feelings were hurt. Her face turned red, and she bowed her head in disappointment. Her six toed feet were flapping in the air.

"I'm sorry," Pierce said realizing his roughness. "We're all a little on edge," he explained to the pint sized fairy with the odd looking feet.

"It's quite all right. Felicia is going to help you out in every way that she can," Felicia explained in the third person.

"What do we need?" Skip asked.

"Well, it looks like we need to be dressed in black, and we need to bring the back packs," Pierce said looking around at their gear.

"Other things may appear as we need them," Felicia hinted.

"What do you mean?" Skip asked.

"You'll see in due time, my Dear," Felicia said politely.

Chapter 4.4
Ready?

S kip walked into her room and came out with her Book of Spells. When dropping it into the leather pack, she realized it still felt empty. Felicia gave a smile and a little wink.

All three teenagers got dressed appropriately for their mission, grabbed their backpacks, and headed for the double doors. They were followed by one tiny fairy with six toes on each foot and a major attitude. There wasn't time for an explanation for the bad mood.

Making their way quietly down the long spiral staircase, they took a left toward the entrance. The once busy hallway was now empty and quiet. One might call it eerie.

During the silent walk down the hallway, they couldn't help but notice the pictures of the three member teams on the wall. The picture with the black cloth was still there as well. Doug was dying to ask Felicia what she knew about the covered picture, but he had other priorities. The hallway was lit by candles, because any power the castle used to hold was now gone. The energy source was tapped dry, and the future of the castle was in the hands of Skip Corbin, Doug Manion, Pierce Butterworth, and Felicia the fairy. They took one final look at the four old pictures of their parents, all which seemed to be saying good luck. Something about the facial expressions in the picture had changed. There seemed to be a look of seriousness. Oddly, upon closer inspection, all the pictures on the vast wall had the same look.

Doug, Skip, Pierce, and Felicia made their way out the door. When they walked a quarter mile toward the gate, Skip looked up and saw Baron Doha in the lookout. Their eyes met, and he smiled and nodded. Doha looked very solemn. It made all four of the adventurers nervous. They took a right out the entrance, and walked along the thick green grass toward the forest. At night though, the green grass looked a shade of black. It was a color that the four travelers had to get used to.

"Pick that up, we'll need it," Felicia said, pointing toward an unlit torch.

"Things don't just get dropped around here," Doug thought to himself. Skip picked it up and held it in her hand. Pierce went to light it, but Doug stopped him.

"Not now. We should conserve our tools until we really need them. We have the stars tonight," he said.

Skip and Pierce looked up. They had never noticed the stars before, but this night was different. The stars seemed to shine down on them as if each tiny one was looking out for each of the children and the fairy.

With every step taken, they felt more psyched for the mission. Pierce looked over and smiled at everyone else. The others smiled back. Not a happy smile, but one that showed contentment about the decision to leave a day early.

Eisenhut stood in the bushes unseen, next to the castle wall. They were too focused on the mission to see him. Eisenhut wasn't allowed to enter the forest, but he was allowed to guard them up until they walked into it. And guard them was exactly what he had in mind. These three were special to him. They were from Waterville. It was Eisenhut's hometown, and the place that grew the best Hide-and-Seekers in the world.

A few minutes later the four gem seekers made their way into Shadow Forest and disappeared from Eisenhut and Doha's view.

PART III SHADOW FOREST

Chapter 5.0 The Search Begins

T he weather changed as soon as they entered the boundary that separated Shadow Forest from Sangerfield. It dropped at least twenty degrees, and the three teenagers looked at each other.

"Aren't you cold?" Skip asked Felicia as they began to add layers to their chilled bodies.

"No, I don't feel temperature. Do you think I would dress like this if I did?" she asked. They knew she had a point, considering she was wearing a sequined dress that didn't have sleeves.

"Where do we begin?" Pierce asked.

"I'm not sure," Doug said.

"Why don't you check your compass?" Felicia suggested.

"What compass?" Doug asked, thinking he forgot to pack something.

"The one in your bag," she told him, with a focused look on her face as if he was supposed to understand exactly what she was talking about. Doug reached into his bag and grabbed an antique gold compass that was a bit tarnished.

"How did you know that was in there?" Doug asked.

"My...Lord Eisenhut made sure you had everything you needed,"

Felicia answered. "Ludicrous lives in the north, and that is where we have to go," she explained.

"Why didn't we know this beforehand?" Pierce asked anxiously.

"Because kids never learn anything unless they know it will affect them. Lord Eisenhut wanted to you to be hands-on learners. I consider this hands-on," Felicia said flatly.

"Plus, you were learning so much at the beginning, we figured we would tell you as you go," she explained.

"One more question," Skip asked.

"Caw, caw," the sound of a bird was heard flying overhead.

Skip looked up and never thought twice that it was a lone crow, like the lone crow that flew over them during the Castle Cup. Felicia looked up and shivered at the sight of the bird, because she didn't want to be its dinner.

"It would be just like Ludicrous to try that on me," Felicia said to herself. "You had a question Skip."

Skip looked at Felicia after looking at the crow. On the list of important things, the crow was not important enough to take time to ask questions about. Besides, Ludicrous Zwevil knew that the three were in the forest. She knew everything that happened in her forest.

"Oh yeah," Skip tried to remember what she was going to ask. "If you have to be a teenager to enter the forest, how is it you can come in?" she asked.

Pierce and Doug stopped in their tracks and waited for the answer. It was a question they never thought of, but it was a good one.

"Simple," Felicia began. "I'm too small to notice. I'm under the radar," and with that she flew off.

"Works for me," Pierce said.

Skip looked up to find the crow, and noticed that it flew off screaming its "caw" toward the dark distance in the woods. It flew north.

Over to their right, eyes watched them, and a chill swept over the travelers' bodies. Skip, Doug, and Pierce began to sense danger. Although the whole mission was going to be dangerous, it was easy to sense.

"Are you ready to run?" Doug whispered.

The three others nodded their heads.

"On three," he said quietly.

Rustling began in the bushes.

"One," Doug started.

More rustling around, and more than one creature was causing it. The noise got louder and something began running their way.

"Two," Doug continued remaining calm.

As they slowly walked a few more steps, the creature ran toward them. Footsteps hard against the leafy ground.

"Three," Doug yelled in a whisper, and the three broke out into a sprint to a big oak tree about fifty yards ahead of them.

Felicia kept up as they ran. Flying was easier than running. Behind them, two forest trolls sprinted out of the bushes. Skip got a glance at them and could not believe how ugly the two creatures were. Their greasy dark hair was flying wildly as they ran after the three children, and saliva dripped from their mouths. Two big yellow teeth hung on both ends of their gaping jaws, and they stood about four feet tall, even with their stumpy legs, they moved fast, getting more speed with each step taken.

Doug, Skip, Pierce, and Felicia made it behind the tree, and peeked out to see the trolls coming quickly toward them.

"Hold my hand," Doug commanded, and his two friends grabbed on, as Doug closed his eyes to think about the safety they needed desperately. Suddenly, all three teenagers disappeared.

"Felicia, grab me" Doug's invisible voice whispered to save her, but he no more got out the words and Felicia disappeared as well. "I guess she has her own necklace," Doug thought to himself.

The gnomes walked confused around the tree grunting at each other. Doug felt like he was wrapped in a big warm blanket that kept danger at bay. The trolls walked around, and even at one point walked right through the three scared travelers. Felicia hovered above them.

"Wer'd they gho?" one said to the other.

"You let 'em gho," the other yelled, snapping at the other.

They violently beat each other while looking. One of the creatures pushed the other right toward Doug, Skip, and Pierce, and the three invisible teenagers closed their eyes terrified by the thought of the troll breaking them apart. Skip envisioned the gnomes having her for dinner with an appetizer of Pierce. Gripping each other tightly, the troll just fell through where their bodies were taking up invisible space.

Nothing happened, and the gnomes had no idea where the three humans were. The necklace of invisibility not only made them impossible to see, it also made them unattainable to touch.

Skip picked up a rock with her free hand from behind the creatures. Doug and Pierce couldn't say anything because they didn't want to be heard, but they thought Skip was losing her mind. Staring at Doug as if to tell him it would be ok, she threw the rock hard toward a bush about twenty yards away. All three children, and Felicia watched as the rock slowly flew through the air. As it hit the bushes, it made a rustling noise. The trolls looked over and saw nothing. There was a look of confusion on the faces of the ugly creatures. Or perhaps that was just their normal expression. One nudged the other one, gesturing to go toward the bush.

Even though at first they were freaking out when Skip picked up the rock, Pierce and Doug could tell what Skip's plan was. Pierce picked up more rocks with his free hand and hurled them toward the bushes. The rocks flew even further, and the gnomes began to run toward to the bushes where the noise came from. Totally confused by the noise, the trolls looked around each bush hoping the three humans would suddenly appear.

Another rock flew further, but none of the teenagers threw it. Felicia had flown ahead to throw the trolls off their trail, dropping rocks along the way. The wand in her hand gave her the ability to rustle the rocks together as she flew over them. The trolls followed the sound of the rocks like lost puppies.

"Good idea," Doug said.

"I thought we were dead," Pierce said back.

"I thought they could see our footprints," Skip asked.

"They can," Felicia said reappearing over them, but they can't grab you. They go through. That was my idea to add to the features of the necklace," she said proudly.

"Time to move on to the cave," Doug said, knowing there was no time for rest.

He quickly came back into sight, touching the necklace as if to say thank you. Getting up, they walked north toward where they hoped the gem would be. Skip looked up to catch a second glimpse of the stars, but they were nowhere to be seen. All she could see was darkness, because tree-made canopies covered the forest ceiling. One lone crow flew over their heads, and Felicia knew it was following them.

Noises filled the dead air, and the explorers tried their best not to be scared. Every step they took, leaves crumbled underneath them.

"This is not like the woods in Gardner Park," Doug said to the other three.

"Gardner Park has never been as scary as this," Skip agreed.

"Sure it has," Pierce argued.

His two best friends and the one lone fairy looked at him for an explanation as they made their way through the forest.

"Listen. It's simple. If we think this is like Gardner Park, then we'll think it's like home and we'll be less scared while we're here," he reasoned.

"How do you plan on doing that?" Doug asked.

"We focus," Pierce said.

"Imagine you're home, and focus on getting the Gem of Gicalma like you would focus on getting the Faux Diamond," Pierce coached.

"I guess we have nothing to lose," Doug said in agreement.

Skip and Doug figured they would give Pierce's suggestion a try, because they weren't going to be going home, either to Waterville or Sanger Castle until they found the gem. Their focus changed from a life or death situation, to a game of Hide-and-Seek. It became a more optimistic challenge.

"Felicia. I have a question," Skip said.

"What's that my dear?" Felicia answered.

"Can trolls usually talk in English?" she asked.

"They spoke English?" Pierce asked.

Doug gave the same look as if he didn't know that trolls could talk either. Skip was the only one who heard them.

"You didn't hear them?" Skip asked everyone.

"No," Doug and Pierce answered.

"Actually, you're the only one who understood them," Felicia explained. Skip was definitely confused. "You can understand Gnome," she said to Skip.

"I can?" Skip said completely taken aback.

"It's one of your gifts. You can understand different languages, and Gnome is one of them," she explained.

Skip looked up to the canopy of trees, again feeling special for being able to understand trolls. Looking up to the trees she was hoping to see stars, or the moon. Nothing was there, not even the crow. She wanted some example of the outside world to free her from feeling trapped in the forest.

A strange looking bird flew over within her eyesight, but it wasn't the crow. She had never seen such a beautiful bird filled with such bright colors. The wingspan was the size of Skip's body. Feeling comforted by the unfamiliar new bird, Skip forged ahead a little more bravely. Something about the bird reminded her of home.

"Shhh," Pierce whispered.

"We didn't say anything," Doug answered.

Pierce glared over at Doug. They stood motionless.

"Over in the..." before Pierce finished the words, an enormous snake's head slithered out of the bushes followed by its gigantic long leathery body.

They never saw it coming. Pierce and Doug froze with fear. Skip jumped out of the way as the snake grabbed her two best friends. Its body began to wrap tightly around them. As they tried to wiggle themselves out of the tight hold, the snake strengthened its muscles, squeezing tighter.

"Ahh!!! Help," they screamed. "I can't breathe," Doug screamed, losing his voice in the pain of being squeezed by the thirty-foot long snake.

It's scales gripped tighter, and Pierce could feel his breath being taken away. The squeeze sucked oxygen out of their ribs. Skip jumped back as the tail of the snake lunged at her. The green and black creature with small diamonds all over it tried to capture the third victim in hopes of destroying them all together. It was on a mission to destroy the intruders.

"Let go of my friends or die," Skip screamed as she jumped in the air, grabbing the unlit torch. Her instincts as the guard were coming out. No time for conversation. She lit the torch quickly and held it in the air.

"Hurry," Doug screamed using his last breath.

The flame flew off the torch, and Skip bolted toward the snake.

"Burn," Skip yelled as she stabbed the torch into the snake's scales.

Its head rapidly flew into the air, and flew back down at Skip with its tongue sticking out. Four yellow slimy sword like teeth flew down in her direction. Poisonous venom dripping off each sharp tooth. Turning to the right, she took the torch and jammed it into the snake's mouth. The immense creature slithered about, unwrapping Doug and Pierce, reeling in pain because of the fire burning in its mouth. The victims fell to the leafy ground, passing out from the lack of oxygen and the shock of the moment.

The snake fell to the ground defeated. Skip stood motionless with the remainder of the torch in her hand, after successfully defeating the overgrown diamond headed snake. It lay in front of her dead from the immense burning it endured from the pint-sized Skip.

Skip regained her composure and ran to her fallen friends. It seemed too late.

"Oh no. Please wake up! I can't do this alone. I need you both," she wept over them fearing they met the same fate as the snake.

Felicia fluttered about over Skip's head.

"Do something," Skip yelled in tears at the fairy.

"There is nothing I can do," she replied.

"You're a fairy. Use your magic," Skip screamed.

"Or is there?" she said flying through the air with her hand over her mouth, thinking hard.

"I could use my power of reverse, or my defibulator wand," she said out loud.

"Hurry," Skip yelled desperately.

"Yes, yes, that should work," Felicia said out loud. Although she really meant to say it to herself.

"What should work?" Skip said weeping.

Felicia took out her silver wand, and pointed it toward the two boys. As she was about to perform her magic, Doug and Pierce began coughing uncontrollably. Skip jumped back wondering what to do next.

"You're not dead!" she yelled looking at her two dazed friends as they regained composure.

"What happened?" Pierce asked in between coughs lying on the ground.

"Your guard, guarded you," Felicia simply said to the boys.

"Where did that thing come from?" Doug asked, breathing heavily.

"Many creatures live in here. They have a lot to protect," Felicia warned.

"Thanks Skip," Doug said, grabbing her hand helping himself up from the ground. "Yeah, thanks," Pierce said standing up. "I won't mess with you anymore," Pierce said chuckling, trying to hide his fear.

"Strong women are important," Felicia said, laughing as she began to fly away. "Let's go, we don't have a lot of time," she commanded as if she forgot all about the terrifying experience they just had.

Doug, Skip, and Pierce began to walk slowly, feeling a tighter connection to each other. Doug and Pierce felt indebted to Skip for her heroic actions. They broke into a little jog to catch up to Felicia. The faster they ran away from the lifeless snake, the better. Fear of another snake helped them regain their energy to run a little faster as well.

An hour passed and Skip, Doug, and Pierce kept seeing the same scenery. Felicia had been through there before, and knew it well.

"Are you sure we're going the right way?" Skip asked.

"Yes," Doug replied looking at his compass, then came to a stop. "Doug. I need your help," came an unknown inner voice. "Who said that?" he asked looking around.

"Who said what?" Skip asked, looking over at Pierce, who in return shrugged his shoulders.

"Doug, please hurry. I need you," the voice said again.

"That," Doug said looking at his traveling companions.

"I didn't hear anything," Skip answered.

"Inner voices," Pierce said.

"Someone needs our help," Doug said.

"Are we going the right way?" Skip asked, staring at her cousin.

"We're heading north. Somehow I think we'll know when we get there," he said.

"I have an idea," Felicia said from her place in the air.

The three stopped and looked at her. "How about we find a place to camp for the night," she suggested trying to take Doug's mind of the voice.

"What about the voice?" Doug asked, not knowing what to do.

"You'll be no good to the voice if you're tired," Felicia warned, trying to find time to plan an attack on the cave.

"Where in the world would we sleep?" Pierce asked.

"On the ground, under some camouflage," she said.

"What would we sleep on?" Skip asked.

"You'd be surprised to see what you're carrying," Felicia hinted.

Doug thought it was a good idea to take a break, and he was busy looking around to find a place. They came across a section of huge Redwood Trees, which had bushes all around them.

"How about over there?" Doug suggested.

"What if another creature is around there?" Pierce asked, trying to hide his nervousness.

"That's a chance we'll have to take," Doug said. "Besides, we have Skip. She's our guard," he said flatly.

Skip smiled at the compliment. She had been patiently waiting to see where she would fit in with her two friends. Since they entered Shadow Forest, it had been she who showed the most strength. She felt a sense of pride.

The travelers walked around the tree and scouted out whether any animals had been there. They ducked under the big bushes and found refuge against the tree.

"Open your bags and you'll find what you need," Felicia directed.

Doug opened his black leather bag and much to his amazement, found a black down sleeping bag, and pulled it out. Pierce and Skip did the same thing.

"What will you do?" Skip asked Felicia.

"I require no sleep. I'll be the look-out to give you time to rest," she said to Skip.

"I'm hungry," Pierce whined a little.

"Check your bag," Felicia directed again, realizing that the teens were not catching on yet.

"That's awesome," Pierce said as he pulled out a ham sandwich and bag of chips.

Doug and Skip hurried to look in their bags after they saw the enormous sandwich Pierce received from his leather-giving bag. Skip pulled out a turkey sandwich and an apple, and Doug pulled out a peanut butter and jelly, which was his favorite. There was a banana in his bag as well.

"I'm a little cold," Skip said, slightly worried about sounding like she was a complainer.

"My dear children, get in your sleeping bags, they do more than you could imagine," Felicia said with a smile.

Doug got into his sleeping bag and disappeared.

"Huh?" Pierce said with a confused expression on his face.

"That look is priceless," Felicia said to Pierce and Skip recognizing their confusion. "What is Hide-and-Seek in Shadow Forest without a sleeping bag of invisibility," Felicia asked as if it was something normal.

"We disappear," Skip asked.

"Yes, but you can still see each other, and I can see you, but no one else can," Felicia explained. "That was Henry…I mean Lord Eisenhut's idea," she slipped.

Pierce and Skip slipped into their sleeping bags, too tired to hear Felicia call Eisenhut by his first name, and instantly felt warm and safe. Much to their amazement they could see each other. Their stomachs were full and they were safe for the evening. Exhaustion fell over all of them.

"Take these mints," Felicia ordered. She handed them three tiny mints.

"What are these," Pierce asked.

"They're teeth cleaning mints," she said. "They will instantly clean your teeth, and give you better breath. Which by the way, you sort of need," she said directing her comment toward Pierce. Pierce turned red with embarrassment. He kept breathing into his hand to see if Felicia's comment was true.

The day was filled with excitement, both good and bad, and they needed rest. Sleeping was not going to be a problem for any of them. Felicia fluttered about making sure that her three teenage friends would be safe for the whole night. It was her reason for being there, and she wasn't going to let anything happen to them.

Doug couldn't help but think of the new voice in his head, which he heard several times as he slept. Knowing he had to find Khalil Flatbottom when he reached Zwevil's cave, he hoped that was the voice he was hearing because it meant that Khalil was still alive.

The next morning the three woke up feeling refreshed and ready to go.

"Breakfast would be good," Pierce said out loud.

"Check your bag," Doug said with a smile.

They all reached quickly for their bags and instantly found breakfast waiting for them. Felicia flew above them with a smile, feeling gratified by the work she had done so far. Food was an important energy source for them, and she needed to make sure the three travelers had all the energy they needed. After they finished, Felicia once again handed them a teeth-cleaning mint, and they instantly popped them into their mouths. Pierce kept trying to hide his face as he checked his breath again. Felicia laughed when she noticed him breathing into his hand.

Doug packed his down sleeping bag back into his leather

pack, which was much easier to do than his sleeping bag at home. This one slid back into the bottomless pack without a problem.

"Wow, that was easy," he said.

Pierce and Skip followed suit and did the same thing. Both were amazed by the ease of the situation.

"Too bad the whole trip isn't this easy," Skip said laughing.

"Sometimes you need to take the easy with the hard," Felicia said with wisdom. The three teenagers nodded their heads in agreement. Doug grabbed his tarnished compass out of his pocket.

"We need to go that way," he said pointing north.

"You're the navigator," Pierce said in agreement.

As they proceeded into their journey, questions began to fill their minds. These questions preoccupied them from wondering who might be watching them as they made their way through the tall weeds that grew in the dark forest. Suddenly, taking them by surprise, a snow-white deer ran by them.

"What was that?" Pierce said suddenly stopping.

"Not you, too," Skip said wondering if Pierce could hear voices too?

Pierce turned around and looked but the deer was nowhere in sight. Suddenly, it ran quickly by again, only this time all the travelers saw it.

"It's a deer," exclaimed Skip.

"I've never seen a white deer before," Doug said staring at it with amazement.

"It's a white Stag," Felicia said. "And it's quite rare to find one, but there are a couple in Shadow Forest."

"Does that mean it guards the forest for Zwevil?" Doug asked.

"No, it watches out for the good that travel through the forest. It's watching out for you," Felicia said. Felicia no sooner finished her sentence about the stag and it was gone. It disappeared into the blackness of the forest.

"Why is it always dark in here?" Pierce asked inquisitively as he, Doug, and Skip watched the Stag as it ran out of sight.

"I mean. It's obviously daytime and there isn't any light coming through the trees," he continued.

"It's always dark in here," Felicia said.

"Light isn't allowed in the forest. Not as long as Ludicrous Zwevil is the ruler," she said. Felicia suddenly fell silent after she uttered the words.

"What's wrong?" Skip asked.

"Nothing," Felicia answered.

"No seriously, what's wrong?" Doug asked.

The three walkers stopped in their tracks and stared at the fairy flying in the air.

"It's dark everywhere," Felicia said solemnly.

"Yeah, we know. That's why I asked you," Pierce said, confused by Felicia's hesitation in her explanation.

"No, I mean, it's dark outside of the forest now too," she said waiting to see the reaction she would receive.

"What do you mean?" Doug said with his mouth hanging slightly open.

"I mean, until we get the Gem of Gicalma, there will be no light in our land," she said seriously.

Chills flew up Doug's back at the seriousness of her statement.

"So when they lose energy, they lose it everywhere," Pierce said. "Without the Gem of Gicalma we have many dark days ahead of us in Sangerfield."

"But what about Eisenhut?" Doug asked.

"His gift can only do so much, which is why it is so important to capture the Gem of Gicalma. Without it, we have nothing, and the creatures who live in darkness, have everything," she said.

Thoughts flew through Skip's mind, worried that she may be trapped in eternal darkness if the mission didn't go well. She was happy to think that she could somehow make it back to Waterville, where everything seemed sunny. Then, another thought entered her mind.

"Wait a minute. Are you telling me we can't get back through Toaster Pond either?" Skip said in a panic.

"No," Felicia simply answered.

"Well it would have been nice if someone told us that," Skip said trying to control her heavy breathing.

"We tried. We told you it was serious," Felicia answered.

"Well we didn't realize it was THAT serious," Doug retorted.

"Get the gem and everything will be fine," she said.

"Well if that's all we have to do, let's go," Pierce said sarcastically.

"I have no doubt that you three can do it. We're, I mean, you're from Waterville," Felicia said flatly.

Doug, Skip, and Pierce never thought that being from the small town of Waterville would give them so much power over such an enormously serious situation.

"Since we're batting a thousand with our questions..." Pierce said with a smile. Felicia looked and smiled back.

"What is it?" she asked.

"Why was there a picture that was covered with a black cloth in the hallway in the castle?"

"Oh that's an easy one," she said.

Doug doubted any of this was easy, but he was eager for the answer.

"It is a picture of someone who never returned to Sanger Castle," she began.

"Who is that?" Skip said, sadly hoping their picture wouldn't be covered in the next few days.

"Khalil Flatbottom, Skyler Rogers, and Ali Choukeir" she answered.

"Is that the Baron's son?" Pierce asked.

"Yes, it was. And Khalil is the one we are looking to bring back," Felicia answered.

"Why didn't they ever return to the castle?" Pierce seemed afraid to ask.

"Khalil was about seventeen at the time, and a nice boy, but he wanted to be friends with everyone. He hated that someone might not like him. One day he entered the woods and Ludicrous Zwevil struck up a friendship with him. She actually began to put a spell on him. Knowing full well that Khalil was a good Seeker and would probably be the one coming for the Gem of Sophia, which was a gem we used for a very important portal to England," Felicia said.

"Why did she let him go?" Skip asked.

"Because she needed someone on the inside to make sure the gem would remain safe in the forest," Felicia answered. "If she had Khalil, it meant that the whole team would fail the mission. Khalil was too nice to recognize Ludicrous' bad behavior, and he never told anyone that he met her. Skyler was impressionable, and did everything Khalil wanted her to do. Ali had just turned thirteen and was too brave for his own good. They won the yearly competition and set into the woods one night to capture the gem. However, when they got here, Ludicrous put a spell on Khalil that guaranteed he would be on her side. Skyler's body was found and brought back to the castle, but no one knows what happened to Ali, everyone fears the worst," Felicia said, stopping to a hover in the air.

The three travelers stopped to listen, wondering why they needed to bring back Khalil if he was responsible for the disappearance of the other two.

"They came to get the gem, and because of Khalil's misguided need for friendship, two players were never heard of again. Khalil was trapped in the forest forever, and the gem was not recovered. However, if we can return Khalil to normal, then we find out how to beat Ludicrous, and we may find out what happened to Ali. Khalil was a brilliant student, and if returned to normal, he would make a great addition to the wand at Sanger Castle."

"How was Khalil trapped here?" Doug asked.

"He unfortunately was turned into a beast," she said. "Actually a Juggernaut," she said, not knowing if they knew what one was.

Fortunately for her, Eisenhut had explained some of the information before their trip. Skip looked up into the trees and saw the crow flying around above her.

"What's that?" she was about to point out the crow, but was instantly stopped by a feeling of despair.

There was silence, but only for a moment. Within a few seconds, there was a rustling in the trees that made all of them stop dead in their tracks. What caused the noise was the biggest creature they had ever seen. Skip instantly got ready for a fight, but her instincts told her not to grab the torch. It was something else she needed.

An enormous giant came lumbering out of the bushes into the clearing where Doug, Skip, and Pierce were standing.

"That is a juggernaut," Felicia said to them, as if they cared for a vocabulary lesson at the moment.

Standing at least twenty feet tall, it's arm span was as long as he was tall. He happened to be missing a few teeth in his mouth, but Doug and Pierce were not about to tell him. He grunted once, which even Skip couldn't understand, and began a fast walk toward the three. Grabbing Pierce in one fell swoop, he turned around and laughed at Skip, he kicked dirt in her face. Her strength didn't scare him. She lost her footing and fell. The dirt flew in the air blinding Doug and Felicia as well, knocking Felicia through the dark cold air. By the time the dust cleared, Pierce was gone.

"No!" Skip screamed, looking in the direction of the giant who was running away with a motionless Pierce in his clenched fist.

"That, unfortunately, was Khalil," Felicia said frankly.

Skip was overcome with tears, but as soon as they came, they went.

"He had to be the one who made the noise when we first came here," Skip said remembering their trip out of Toaster Pond. She couldn't believe anything else in the forest was as big as him, or as noisy. Which would make him easy to find.

"Calm down. We'll get him back. Look," Doug said pointing toward the ground.

Khalil was not only seen running to the north, but he left huge footprints in the dirt leaving them a track to follow. Doug had every intention of following the huge footprints until he got his stolen friend back.

Chapter 5.1
Hypnotic

D oug, Skip, and Felicia were silent for a while as they walked north, following Khalil's footprints. Doug was upset, not being able to shake the vision of his best friend being taken away by the giant. Its huge arms lifted Pierce up around its shoulder, and Pierce hit his head on the choker that was wrapped around its neck.

"I have a feeling this won't just lead us to the giant," Doug finally spoke up.

Skip looked at him guessing what he was thinking and hoping that he was right. "You think this is going to lead us to Zwevil," she said.

Doug nodded in agreement.

"Well, at least we'll get it all out of the way at once," Felicia joked trying to lighten the mood.

Felicia was hoping that Pierce only had good thoughts in his head. Those positive thoughts could stop Zwevil from trying to get him on her side and stay in the forest with her. Ludicrous would try to persuade one of them to stay, and get rid of the other two.

"Help! Doug!" came another inner voice. Only this time Doug recognized it as Pierce's. The two had a strong connection and Pierce wanted to use it to his advantage.

"I'm in the cave," he said giving a hint as to his whereabouts.

Suddenly, the voice stopped. Doug looked at Skip and Felicia, but kept Pierce's plea for help to himself. He didn't want Skip unfocused as they went into the cave.

Making their way through the darkened woods was beginning to get frustrating for Doug and Skip. Too much time had gone by without a voice guiding them, and the cool breeze began blowing colder air.

"How are we going to get him back?" Skip asked.

"My job is to seek and yours is to guard," Doug said firmly out loud.

"Huh," Skip said feeling a little slighted by his answer.

Doug realized how he sounded. "We need to think of this like Hide-and-Seek," he said.

"We're here because we won a competition," he began.

"Two actually," Skip chimed in feeling a little more positive.

"We won two Hide-and-Seek competitions, and that's why we're here. Remember what Pierce said. Treat it like the game."

"It's a little more serious than the games we played. We couldn't be killed in those games," Skip said back to Doug.

"Yeah, but all of those games led us up to this. What if Pierce got captured during a Hide-and-Seek game at home?" Doug asked.

"I'm not sure. It never happened," she said.

"Look, you have proven yourself as a guard. Now it's my time to prove myself," he said.

"Yeah, but I let the giant get away," Skip said in return.

"It was a mistake. We're getting used to this still," Doug said trying to boost her self-esteem. "We can't be down right now. Pierce needs us. And he needs both of us," Doug said positively.

"Uh hum," Felicia said from the air.

"He needs all three of us," Doug said.

"Sorry, no offense," he apologized to the pint sized fairy.

"No offense taken," she said back.

The day had flown by and it was getting late. Doug knew they would never make it to their destination, wherever it was, by nightfall.

Suddenly the cold weather brought snow. Like the kind of snowstorm kids wish for around the winter holidays. The flakes fell down peacefully, but thick, wet, and large.

"It's summer, how can it snow?" Doug said , in a trance by the mesmerizing soft wet snow that fell through the canopy of trees.

"It's beautiful," Doug commented as he began to feel tired from the walk.

"It just shouldn't be snowing," Skip added. "It's the middle of summer."

Doug began walking ahead incoherently ignoring every word flowing out of Skip's mouth.

"Yeah, it's beautiful," Doug said again in his trance-like voice.

Felicia and Skip looked at each other trying to figure out why Doug suddenly became despondent when the snow began falling.

"Doug!" Skip yelled, realizing why he was walking ahead repeating himself over and over.

"Yes, it's beautiful," he said again and again.

"Felicia, what do we do," Skip asked.

Felicia needed a moment to think, but she wasn't sure it would work.

"I need you to do this, with the chance that it may hurt him, and not work," she lectured to Skip.

"Great, there's a plan," Skip said back.

Felicia frowned a bit with disappointment in Skip's lack of confidence.

"I'm sorry, yes I'll do it," Skip agreed apologetically.

"Follow my lead and listen for my directions" Felicia said with a look of hope.

She flew up toward Doug, and out of her backpack came a warm blanket, which grew when it hit the air. She took the blanket and wrapped it around Doug.

"It's beautiful," he kept saying to himself staring into the soft white snow.

"Desperate times call for desperate measures," Felicia said out loud. "Sorry Doug," she said quietly.

Felicia turned around and looked at Skip, hoping that Skip would be able to do what she was about to be asked. Skip stared up toward Felicia and knew that her turn had come. She waited for the command.

"I need you to tackle him now, before it gets worse," Felicia directed.

"What?" Skip asked in shock. "I can't tackle him," Skip retorted.

"You can if you want him to live," Felicia said in desperation.

"Here I go," Skip said, quickly mustering up her energy. Breaking into a fast run, she dove toward Doug tackling him to the ground.

"It is beu…oh," Doug yelled hitting the ground hard with his cousin Skip on top of him. "Ow, what was that for," he said rubbing his head from the pain and embarrassment of getting tackled by his cousin, let alone a girl.

"Sorry Doug, it was the only way," Felicia said defending Skip's actions.

"What happened?" Doug asked.

"You were hypnotized by the falling snow," Felicia explained.

"What about me? Why wasn't I?" Skip asked.

"Let's just say you make a good guard," Felicia said.

"She makes a good tackle," Doug remarked.

"No, Doug is a good hider, but he always seeks for the gem, and he's observant to everything around him. Unfortunately, that makes him susceptible to situations like that one," Felicia said referring to the snow.

"So, you're saying Skip isn't very observant," Doug said with a laugh. Skip just stared at him silently, holding back her comment.

"No, she just isn't as observant as you. She doesn't get caught up in her surroundings," Felicia said flatly.

Doug wasn't sure what was worse, to be unobservant, or to get caught up in your surroundings.

"Watch it Manion or I'll tackle you again," Skip warned.

"Perhaps we need to start a football team at Sanger Castle," Doug said with a smile.

"Sure, you can be the cheerleader," Skip answered back with a sarcastic grin.

They walked on feeling a little worn down by the snowy event.

"Felicia, have you ever been here before?" Doug asked, not

believing he never thought of it before.

"Yes," she said with a slight smile.

"Why didn't you say anything?" Skip asked.

"Your grandmother told you no one knows the forest better than me. Weren't you listening?" she retorted, defending herself.

Skip and Doug suddenly remembered the conversation they had with Corbin Gram and Dr. Butterworth in their suite.

"Are we on the right track?" Doug asked.

"Yes," she said.

"Do we need to know anything else you're not telling us?" Skip asked.

As soon as the words came out of Skip's mouth, Doug thought of something. The giant came out and took Pierce. It didn't kill any of them, or hurt them either. It was like the giant knew that it would hurt badly enough if it took a member of the team.

"How did it know where to find us?" Doug thought. "She knows we're coming," he said suddenly, half out loud, and half to himself.

Skip stopped and looked at Felicia, who in return looked gratified that Doug figured something so important out on his own.

"Yes, she does," Felicia answered.

"How?" Skip said feeling very disappointed.

"She has a map that tells her when human intruders are coming," Felicia said.

"Then why didn't the giant grab us in our sleep? It would have been easier," Skip said thinking quickly.

"Unless the sleeping bags make us invisible from her too," Doug said.

Felicia couldn't get a word in if she tried at this point. The six-toed fairy could see the tangent that the two teenagers were on.

"How about the necklace? Does that protect us too?" Doug asked.

"Yes, but remember what Lord Eisenhut told you. They can't see you, but they can see your footprints," she warned.

Feeling tired, they made a camp for the evening and got ready to get some rest for the evening.

Unfortunately for Zwevil, the view of the two children disappeared off the map, because unbeknownst to her, they slipped into the sleeping bags becoming invisible to everyone, except for the ones who shared the down sleeping apparatus. Doug could see Skip, and vice versa, but only the fairy that accompanied them could see them as well.

"How are we going to get Pierce?" Skip asked in a whisper.

"We'll make our way into the castle and think as we go," Doug said realizing it wasn't the best plan, but it was the only one he could think of.

"We should be able to spot a castle easy enough," Skip said.

Felicia made a funny noise at the question.

"It is a castle, right?" Skip asked.

"It's a cave," she answered.

"It doesn't matter," Doug said thinking out loud.

"We have the necklace and we'll use it for as long as we can," Doug said. Then he stopped. The thoughts began flying through his head like birds fleeing a dangerous situation.

"Felicia," he said.

"Yes," she said inquisitively.

"We don't need you here anymore," he began.

"What," Skip said in a loud whisper.

"Pierce needs you more than we do," he said. "You know the way to the cave, and you can't be seen. You said she can see human intruders, and no offense, but you're not human," he said apologetically.

She nodded in agreement without taking offense to his thoughts. Although there were times when she was human.

"Can you make sure Pierce is ok and help him figure out how to take the map? If she can't see us coming, then it will make it much easier to sneak in," Doug said.

Skip smiled at her cousin's thoughts.

"Why didn't I think of that sooner?" he said out loud.

"Because you weren't open to it. Now you are," Felicia responded with a look of wisdom and pride in Doug's clever thoughts. "I knew you three were different," she said before she flew away.

"What do you mean?" Skip asked.

"You three are a team. Even when one of you is missing," she said with a smile. "I knew that when I saw you in Waterville," she said hoping they didn't hear her.

"What do you mean, saw us in Waterville?" Doug asked.

"Nothing. I'll explain later. I have a job to do," she said being coy. "Good luck to you both. Get some sleep and watch out for the snow, Doug," Felicia said with a smile hovering before she took off.

"Good luck," Skip said to her, affectionately, laughing at her comment toward Doug. Felicia nodded a thank you and took off toward the north.

Doug looked over at Skip. "It's just you and me now," he said to her.

"We'll watch out for each other," she said back to him.

"Let's get some sleep," Doug said, feeling good about his plan, but nervous that he was sending his new-found friend into a dangerous situation.

The down sleeping bag felt amazingly warm and comfortable. The two teenagers, who were on the cusp of getting the gem, felt as if they were in their beds back at the castle. The magical sleeping bags had a way of making the outside world go away, and helping the inhabitants feel as if they were safe and secure, which they were, but only for the night. Tomorrow will bring unknown dangers.

Chapter 5.2
Ludicrous

The next morning an air of seriousness hit Doug and Skip. "Today is the day," Doug said, looking over at his cousin.

"We should leave soon," Skip advised.

"I wonder how Felicia did last night," Doug thought aloud.

A voice never woke him up or provided him with the information that he needed. It would be a long time before his inner voices evolved.

Skip's mood was serious and focused, knowing that today would be the day they came face to face with Ludicrous.

Doug and Skip made their way north through the trees, bushes, and leaf covered ground. A chill went up their backs, and Doug could feel that they were getting closer to the cave that was the home of the most evil person he would ever meet in his young life. Skip made her way around a bush and fifty yards in front of them was a rock hill that stood a few hundred feet in the air. Skip stopped in her tracks and Doug was not far behind her. They both stared at the large rock hill. Directly in front of them was an opening to what looked like a cave.

"That's got to be it," Skip whispered.

Doug could feel something behind him, like when his sister Beck tried to sneak up and scare him. The force behind him was much more profound than that of a little sister. And this force was angry over the killing of its brother.

At the same time, Skip saw a shadow form in front of her, and it overtook their shadows on the ground.

"I think we're in trouble," Doug said. They turned around to find another enormous diamond headed snake dripping poisonous venom near where they stood. "Sss. Sssss," it slithered bringing its head high in the air. As quickly as the head went up, it swung back and shot toward them.

"Jump," Skip yelled, grabbing her torch that instantly lit as the Snake's four sharp teeth came flying at her.

Doug made his way to the bushes hoping that Skip would take care of this snake like she did the last one. Without being able to stop, the snake jammed its tongue into the fiery torch and jumped back. Its tail came flying around and Doug jumped from the bush he was standing behind. Skip jumped over it at the same time, just making it over the top. She landed and swung back around with the torch and jammed it into the snake's throat burning a hole into it. The snake instantly disintegrated at the touch of the fire, disappearing into the air. Much like the snake from the day before.

Skip stood back sweating at the battle, and Doug felt a sigh of relief come over him as he caught his breath.

"Wow, that was amazing," he said complimenting her brute strength.

"Thank you," she said coolly as if she had no doubt that she could destroy the beast.

"How did you do that?" Doug asked his pint-sized cousin.

"I took the herbs that Fahlzalot gave me," she said. "Chamomile and Cedar Wood gave me the strength I needed. Remember when she explained that the herbs would only work for me?" Skip said, knowing full well that Doug would have asked her for some.

"You have to be careful with herbs. Fahlzalot gave me directions in the pouch, that were written strictly for me," she said out of breath. "Let's go though, we need to keep moving," Skip said.

Doug's eyebrows rose at his cousin's determination and focus. Although he was a little bummed that he couldn't take the herbs. However, he knew he had a necklace of invisibility and heard inner voices, even though they hadn't spoken to him in quite some time.

Doug and Skip took a deep breath and slowly entered the cave. There were torches lit along the wall.

"Put yours down and grab another one," Doug suggested.

"No way," Skip said. "This is my lucky torch."

They anxiously walked down the corridor wondering what lay ahead of them.

Hoping that their other friends had been successful in their missions, they walked slowly toward an open room, which looked like an office. Both were surprised by the fact that it wasn't better guarded.

"Perhaps we weren't expected to make it this far," Doug thought to himself.

They walked close to the walls hoping to be the one offering the surprise, instead of being surprised like they were with the diamond headed snake. Skip walked through the torch-lit room, a little too close to a picture hanging on the wall. Knocking it off its hooks, the picture flew down toward the ground, and Doug reached down and caught it before it crashed to the floor.

"Whew, that was close," Skip said.

"Be careful where you walk," Doug suggested in a parental tone.

They continued to slowly make their way around the room, and Doug motioned toward the desk to check its contents.

As Doug walked, he felt a buzzing in the air. He kept waving his hand to knock whatever insect it was away from his ear.

"Watch it," a familiar voice said.

It was Felicia. She appeared right in front of them. Doug and Skip smiled instantly.

"Where have you been?" they asked.

"Where you told me to go," she answered.

"We're so glad to see you," Skip said.

"Skip just destroyed another snake outside," Doug bragged.

Skip had a look of contentment and fear on her face all at the same time. Doug knew that she was probably sick of battling the enormous snakes. He also knew he owed her his life, for a second time.

"I don't care if I ever see another snake again," Skip wished aloud.

"Where is Pierce?" Doug asked.

"Down the corridor," Felicia answered.

"We thought we'd see you before now," Skip said to Felicia.

Felicia wanted to help but she was under orders. She had a difficult decision to make, but it was one she trusted wholeheartedly.

"I need to let you both work this out. I'm only here to help," she said in return.

Doug and Skip felt confident that they could find Pierce. Suddenly, they heard a woman yelling from another room.

"YOU"LL TALK BOY," the woman's voice screamed.

"I WON'T TELL YOU ANYTHING," Pierce screamed back at her.

Doug and Skip were thankful that their friend was still alive. Slowly making their way toward the two, they peeked around the corner and saw a woman about six feet tall, with light blonde hair. She was wearing a black robe and black combat boots. In her hand was a black staff, which she was pointing in the direction of the too-familiar giant, and the nervous-looking boy with black hair behind iron bars. The staff was about six feet long, sleekly designed and had an imposing presence. Doug, Skip, and Felicia weren't sure whom the staff was being pointed at, but it didn't matter, because the situation looked dangerous. Doug knew he had to act fast.

He grabbed his necklace, closed his eyes and disappeared. Making his way slowly and quietly around the inside perimeter of the cave, he wanted to try to knock the staff out of Zwevil's hand. Bravery took over any ounce of worry he had, because his best friend needed to be saved.

Skip watched as the giant made his way across the room and grabbed at the air. She wasn't sure what Khalil was doing, but she was hoping it didn't involve Doug. All of a sudden Doug appeared in the air, gasping for breath. Khalil wasn't saying a word; he just stared blankly at Doug.

"Ah ha," Ludicrous screamed, as if she knew he was there all along. "That's two. Now where is number three?" she yelled looking around the cave.

Slowly turning to take in every ounce of space in the cave, she couldn't find the one last person she was looking for.

"This is going to be easier than I thought," Ludicrous let out an arrogant laugh.

Unfortunately for Doug, the cave floor was dirty, and his feet made prints as he tried to sneak up on Ludicrous. Khalil's keen eye spotted the footprints going across the cave floor, and now Doug was within his grasp. Khalil had stronger gifts than the trolls from the forest. Doug thought that Khalil's hands would go right through his invisible self, but he was wrong. Perhaps dead wrong.

"Let him go!" Pierce yelled, trying to scare the giant who was four times his size. Skip stood frozen trying to think of something to do.

"SHUT UP, BOY," Ludicrous screamed at Pierce and a flash came out of her staff. Suddenly, Pierce stood frozen like a statue.

Doug's body was limp in Khalil's hand, and Ludicrous was still staring around looking for Skip. Skip was ducking down behind a table, trying to quickly come up with a plan, but also holding in her desire to cry because of the deadly events taking place.

Holding back the tears, the brave girl from Waterville reached deep down into her backpack and found the pouch holding the mirror. She knew she would only have a few seconds to get Khalil's attention. Enough time to show him his reflection, hoping that Eisenhut had been absolutely right that it would work.

Looking around trying to find Felicia, she got the six-toed fairy's attention. Skip gave Felicia a look and the fairy quickly understood what she was supposed to do. Within a second Felicia disappeared. Skip hoped that her silent plan would work and that Felicia understood what to do. There was a loud crash in another room, and it echoed through the dark and damp cave.

"Hold him, and I'll get the girl," Ludicrous commanded her giant slave. Khalil stood in his place, holding Doug in his hand. Loosely enough so Doug could breath, but tightly enough that he couldn't talk. All Doug could concentrate on was a blurry vision of Pierce, and the silver choker Khalil wore around his neck.

"Hey, look," were the only two words that Skip got out of her mouth, too preoccupied with staying safe to come up with a better phrase.

It was enough to get Khalil's attention. He stared down at the little girl, and began to pick his foot up, which was all he needed to squash her. Under Ludicrous's spell, Khalil made no good decisions. Death and destruction were all he knew. As he began to take a step, he was distracted by the strange shiny mirror in Skip's hand.

"Focus now,

Upon this view.

Return you back,

To the human you," Skip said as Ludicrous came running back into the room. "STOP RIGHT THERE," Ludicrous said in a loud piercing scream. "How dare you come into my castle without my knowing."

However, it was too late, because as she finished screaming at Skip, Khalil shrunk down to a man of about six feet tall. His once greasy and dirty hair turned blonde, and he stood wearing a black robe with soft purple triangles on it. The same garb he wore when he blindly entered the forest many years earlier.

"NO," Ludicrous screamed and lunged at Skip, who in return jumped out of the way just in time.

Doug dropped to the floor holding his neck trying to get a breath. Skip jumped back up to her feet, and Ludicrous Zwevil ran at her, with her staff in hand.

Doug's eyes focused on the once-tight choker that fell off Khalil when he shrunk. He noticed that the side that once faced Khalil's large muscular throat, was a little green gem. Khalil grabbed the gem before Doug got to it. Giving it an odd stare, Khalil looked as if he finally felt like he had power. A smile formed on his face and he handed the tiny, but powerful green gem over to Doug. Khalil didn't say a word, still unable to talk from his years as Ludicrous's silent slave.

Doug took the gem and ran toward Ludicrous hoping that his instinct would be correct. Before she could turn around to throw a flash of her staff at Doug, he jumped on her.

"Ahh," Ludicrous yelled, and Doug heard a burning sound, but didn't know where it originated from. Looking down, Doug saw the Gem of Gicalma burning the sleeve of Ludicrous's robe. The staff flew out of her hand and Skip grabbed it. It shrank in her tiny hands. Knowing that magical staffs never work the same in two gifted people's hands, Skip hid it in her backpack and ran over to Pierce.

"LET ME GO!"

Ludicrous screamed, breaking free from Doug who was still burning her with the Gem of Gicalma.

As Ludicrous broke free, she flew through the cave out of sight. Much like a deflating balloon flies through the air. Felicia watched as Ludicrous flew by screaming from the pain of being burned by her most precious possession. And within seconds, Ludicrous was gone.

Khalil walked over to Pierce, and touched his face. His warm, gentle, average sized hands were no longer callused and huge. Doug watched as Khalil closed his eyes, and Pierce became unfrozen. So many powers floated around Sangerfield and Shadow Forest. Khalil seemed determined to finally use his powers for good.

"What happened?" Pierce said coming out of a daze.

"You were put under a spell by Ludicrous," Khalil explained. His voice soft and low.

"Who are you?" Pierce asked. Pierce was frozen during the time that Skip showed the Mirror of Truth to Khalil.

"I'm Khalil Flatbottom," he introduced himself letting Pierce out of his frozen prison.

Pierce stood staring at him. Completely taken over by the idea that they had almost completed their mission.

"Thank you for freeing me," Khalil said looking toward Skip.

"You're welcome. We're glad you're back," Skip said.

"I'm sorry to rush you, but we have to go," Felicia said to the four saviors.

Doug, Skip, Pierce, and Khalil did not have to be told twice, and they made their way out of the cave. All four of them kept looking over their shoulders, making sure Ludicrous didn't sneak up on them.

"I wouldn't worry about her," Felicia said referring to Ludicrous Zwevil. "We won't be seeing her for a very long time. But the Gem is special. We need to get it to Sanger Castle right away."

As they walked through the forest, there was a lot of conversation about their short, but eventful experience in the cave.

"Why did the Gem of Gicalma burn her?" Doug said tightly gripping the gem in his hand.

"The gem represents everything good about Sangerfield. It always stayed with me, because Ludicrous' evilness didn't allow her to touch it," Khalil explained. "She wanted it hidden from Eisenhut, but could never hold it in her own hands," he said.

"Why didn't it burn you?" Skip asked, referring to the fact that Khalil was under a spell and was pretty evil himself.

"Because Khalil was inherently good, and the gem could sense that," Felicia explained.

There was some more silence as they walked through the woods toward Sanger Castle. A long trip behind them, and a long walk ahead of them. Pierce, Doug and Skip weren't thrilled to stay another night in the forest, but they were happy they had their backpacks to make the night a bit better.

"How did we do back there?" Doug asked Felicia as they were walking.

"Very well. Very well indeed," she complimented. "Put the gem in your bag," Felicia said to Doug. "We still need to make our way out of the forest," she said as they walked.

"It's lighter outside," Pierce observed out loud.

The rest of the travelers noticed the light too.

"Let me guess, because of the gem," as he responded to his own question before anyone else could.

"That's correct," Felicia agreed.

"How long will it take us to get back?" Doug asked.

"Not as long as it took us to get here. All of the creatures are in hiding," she said.

"Not that one," Skip said pointing in the air.

Felicia smiled.

"Why are you smiling?" Skip asked.

"That's Mammoth," Felicia explained.

"It's Eisenhut's Hawk," she said.

"It looks nicer than the crow," Skip commented.

"You have a good sense of good and evil Skip," Felicia complimented.

Doug and Pierce were pretty impressed with Skip's fierceness. They made the long walk toward the castle. The sky was brighter and Skip could see the sun. Pierce glanced back behind them, and noticed that there was darkness hanging behind but not over them.

"The forest is still a dangerous place. There have been many children lost for the cause of the gifted, and there will be many more missions taken in the forest to find them," Felicia said.

"Felicia?" Doug began to ask her a question.

"Yes, Doug," Felicia answered.

"Why only one covered picture in the hallway, if there are many lost children?" It occurred to Doug that the lost children were not forgotten in spirit, but were forgotten in pictures. Perhaps if he, Skip, and Pierce saw their faces, they would be able to save them too.

"There are many children who did not heed the warning to stay out of Shadow Forest. They snuck in here during the night, which was a grave mistake," Felicia said sadly.

For a few moments after her story, the travelers were silent. Suddenly, Khalil stopped in his tracks, and the three teenagers stopped behind him. They sensed Khalil tenseness at possible danger ahead. What Khalil saw was the total opposite of danger.

"Look," Khalil said pointing toward two white stags walking toward them.

"What do they want from us?" Doug asked holding his backpack a little tighter.

"To give you a ride," Felicia said.

"What?" Pierce asked, looking at the stags standing in front of him and then at Felicia.

"There will be no need to spend another night in the forest," Felicia said. "They will get you to the castle quickly."

Doug put his hand out in front of the nose of one of the stags, to let it smell his hand and know that Doug meant no harm. However, Doug really had no need to do that because it knew that Doug was safe.

Pierce and Skip did the same thing, and Khalil got up on the stag that Doug was petting.

"Get on this one. Pierce and Skip get on the other," Khalil said.

"What about Felicia?" Skip asked.

"I'll be fine. I have my own way of getting back," she said, and suddenly disappeared without ever saying goodbye.

The four humans held on tight, and the white stags began to hover over the ground, quickly making their way through the forest. Doug held on tight to both the stag and his backpack. He was overwhelmed by the feeling of success he had on the adventure to capture the Gem of Gicalma, and began smiling uncontrollably. Skip and Pierce had the same feeling, and smiled too.

Eager to get the gem back to the castle, they were happy at how fast the two snow-white stags could fly. Three of the four could not wait for the celebration that awaited them. The adult accompanying them felt thankful to have another chance at life. Knowing he owed everything to three teenagers from Waterville who didn't even know him.

PART IV A NEW BEGINNING

Chapter 6.0 Welcome Home

Skip, Doug, Pierce, and Khalil made their way through the forest.

"What will happen when we get back to the castle," Doug asked, as they flew through the air.

"If I remember correctly, Eisenhut puts on a celebration that will blow you away," Khalil said with a smile.

"The forest isn't as scary anymore," Skip commented.

"I know. It seems silly that we were that scared before," Doug added.

Pierce kept his mouth closed in fear that another giant might come out of the trees and grab him.

"Ahh, it seems safer because you were successful in your task," Khalil said.

Skip was confused. Khalil wanted to make his point clearer after seeing the looks on their faces. "Today is bright, because Ludicrous Zwevil is in hiding. She'll be out soon, with more deadly spells up her sleeve," Khalil warned, knowing full well how dangerous Ludicrous could be.

"But I have her staff," Skip said reaching into her bag.

The staff was gone. It was nowhere to be found.

"I put it in there," Skip said, as the other three looked at her.

"Ludicrous controls her staff. She has it in her possession, as you will notice the next time you meet up with her," Khalil warned.

The three teenagers knew he was right, and they hoped that they would be ready again, the next time.

Doug could see the light coming through the break in the tree line and the edge of the forest, as the stags landed on the ground. They were fifty yards away from the open trail back to the castle.

"Why are we stopping?" Doug asked.

"This is where their journey ends," Khalil said referring to the stags. Skip, Doug, and Pierce got off the stags and walked over to pet their noses.

"Thank you," Doug whispered to the snow-white animals.

As they turned around to walk into the open field, the two stags flew away, back into the forest. Felicia flew through the air finding herself quite happy that they were leaving the forest behind.

"Felicia, where did you come from?" Pierce asked.

"The same place you did," Felicia said, not giving any more information. "Zwevil won't be able to see any intruders now," Felicia remarked as they walked along the path to the castle.

"What do you mean?" Doug asked.

She took the Intruder Map out of her bag and handed it to Doug.

"This can't be the actual size," he asked.

"Yes. Such powerful things just seem bigger in your mind," Felicia answered.

"Felicia," Pierce said, with a tone more suited for a parent than a teenager.

"Oh, all right," she said knowing her joke was over.

Felicia looked around at her newfound friends and said, "You have to promise me that you will keep this to yourself."

"Keep what…the map?" Pierce asked.

"No, what I'm about to say," she said.

"I think we have proven ourselves as worthy," Doug interjected.

Felicia knew he had a good point. She tapped the map with her wand and said, *In front of all our eyes, Return the map to its normal size.*"

And suddenly the map grew so big that it nearly fell out of Felicia's tiny hands. Doug caught it in time and took it from her.

"Keep it as a souvenir," Felicia said.

"Won't Eisenhut want it?" Doug asked.

"He doesn't know about it and I think you've earned it," she answered.

"Aren't you worried you'll get in trouble with him if he finds out?" Pierce asked.

"He should be more worried about getting in trouble with me," she said bravely. It sounded as if the old arrogant Felicia who they first met was coming back. Pierce, Doug, and Skip laughed at her obvious joke. Khalil stayed quiet as they made their way to the castle.

"What's wrong?" Skip asked.

"I hope I'm welcome," he answered.

"You will be," Felicia said, flying over his shoulder.

Khalil smiled a bit, but was still nervous that Eisenhut would not be happy to see him.

They heard someone yell something in the distance, but it was muffled. They knew they were close to the castle. The three kids began running down the trail in the direction of Sanger Castle. Felicia flew behind them, and Khalil walked slowly.

"I can't believe we got it," Doug said with a smile to himself in anticipation of what he was about to see. They felt the world fall off their shoulders as they ran down the dirt trail toward the noise.

Suddenly, they rounded a corner, and the cause of the noise multiplied, and the sheer mass of the crowd came into focus. Lined up against the bottom of the wall, and on top of it, stood every teenager, professor and baron that made Sanger Castle their home.

"They're here," Lord Eisenhut announced proudly in a voice that would make a room fall silent.

Instead, the crowd cheered louder as the three teenagers and one fairy made their way closer to the castle. There was a wave of colors in front of them. Every boy and girl wore their competition jerseys, and the adults were in their dark celebratory robes.

"Wow," was all Doug could say as his cheeks turned red with embarrassment.

Corbin Gram and Dr. Butterworth ran up and embraced the

new heroes, and the crowd went wild with applause. The three teenagers felt like celebrities. Khalil walked up the trail with his head down. Eisenhut walked up to Khalil first.

"Welcome home," he said with a warm smile.

And gave Khalil a hug. Khalil's tense shoulders dropped, and he felt happy to be home.

Children were waving and cheering loudly for what seemed like forever. It was overwhelming to the travelers who just exited the forest. After a few more minutes of applause, Lord Eisenhut spoke to the castle residents.

"Ladies and Gentlemen, please calm down. I know how excited you are," he began. The crowd quieted down in anticipation of the speech they were about to hear. "We have the Gem of Gicalma," Eisenhut continued, and the crowd exploded in applause. "This is cause to celebrate," he began holding up his hands. They all knew it was going to be a celebration like no other.

"We shall meet in the dining hall in three hours for a feast," he said with a smile. "We need to give our heroes some time to rest and reacquaint themselves with our castle hospitality," he said with a smile.

Eisenhut walked up to Doug, Skip and Pierce, reaching out, he shook hands with each one, and winked toward Felicia. She turned red with embarrassment from the gesture of gratitude given to her by Eisenhut.

"Tonight, you will be given a Medal of Honor to show our gratitude to you for your bravery," he said. "We cannot thank you enough for what you did. Getting a gem is difficult, and getting the Gem of Gicalma seemed impossible to many, but not to you. You have saved the castle and cemented our goal of opening up the castle as a school in the fall. We would be honored if the three of you would attend as guests of honor," he said to them.

Doug, Skip, and Pierce were speechless. Then Doug thought about his parents for a moment.

"I have to ask permission first," he said.

Skip and Pierce nodded. Pierce was fortunate enough to have his father standing right next to him.

"You have my permission," Duncan Butterworth said to his son.

Pierce could not have been happier. The whole experience was overwhelming, and a dark and dangerous part of it was behind him.

"I trust you will have your parents' permission as well, but it is very responsible of you both to wait to hear it from them," Eisenhut said.

"I would expect nothing less from you," he added proudly.

Holding the gem in his hands, Doug handed the precious jewel to Lord Eisenhut and he beamed with delight. "This is the best thing to ever happen to Sanger Castle. Horatio Sanger and my father, Vernon, would be proud of this moment," he said looking as if he was about to weep.

"May I ask a question?" Doug said.

"Of course," Eisenhut replied.

"Why did it take so long to turn this into a school?" Doug asked as if it was a simple question.

"Ahh, yes. Not an easy question," Eisenhut began. "I was nervous about starting a school because of the Zwevils first and foremost. But starting a school also takes a lot of time, and you have to make sure you have the right wand, and that you can get enough gifted students to join. It's like starting a business. You have to get the word out," Eisenhut explained. "We started with summer classes and tournaments, and then started finding top notch professors. Word of mouth is everything. Suddenly, more and more children began attending the castle during the summer, and we knew there would be enough for enrollment. Then we began losing energy. And getting the gem was the solution to help regain that energy."

Eisenhut paused for a moment of reflection. Looking up at the crowd of children and adults who were celebrating in their own way. His voice broke. "Now we have what we need. No more obstacles…for now." And with that, he needed to move on.

"We need to put this in its place," he commanded, and Parker Gardner walked up to assist him. "Please go with your grandmother and father back to your suites to relax before the feast," Eisenhut suggested.

"We can talk more another time," he said with a grin.

Doug, Skip, and Pierce nodded, feeling happy with the thought of relaxing for a few hours. Khalil stood waiting for Eisenhut to finish.

"One last thing," Eisenhut said as they were walking away. They turned and looked at him. "What do you think of our bags?" he said with a smile.

"Can we keep them?" Pierce asked.

"Of course," Eisenhut smiled, obviously giving the answer Pierce was looking for.

"Oh," Pierce stopped and turned toward Eisenhut.

"You can have this back," he said beginning to take off his necklace. "It didn't work well for me," he said feeling a bit bad about trying to use it for the first time on Zwevil.

Doug and Skip had no idea that Pierce had tried to use the mind-altering necklace. Lord Eisenhut smiled and put up a hand to say stop.

"It will," he said with a smile, as if he could see the future.

Floating away, like all Eisenhut's are known to do, Khalil followed along in the same fashion. Doug, Skip, and Pierce looked at each other not saying a word about Eisenhut's response.

"Let's go get you cleaned up and into better clothes," Corbin Gram said with a smile. The three teenagers were filthy from their adventure.

"I'm proud of you," Dr. Butterworth whispered to his son.

A warm feeling came over Pierce. He felt proud of himself too.

"We didn't get Zwevil though," he said to his Dad.

"Someday you might," his Dad answered. Skip and Doug overheard the conversation.

"We're not done, are we?" Doug asked inquisitively.

"I don't think so," Corbin Gram answered.

"You all are special. You're the gifted ones," she said. "You'll do great things here."

The three teenagers made their way down the hallway and up the spiral staircase.

"Congratulations," a British voice said as they all walked

into their suite. Baroness Choukeir was delivering flowers to their room.

"You made us very proud," she said happily.

Although she seemed in good spirits, she also looked like she was holding something back. Doug looked at her and knew what she was thinking.

"I'm sorry we didn't find Ali," he said, hoping he wasn't out of line. Baron Choukeir melted at Doug's words.

"Thank you Dear. Someday you may, though," she said with a smile. "I have faith in all of you," she said. There was a pause in conversation, where words were not necessary.

"Now, now. No time for this serious talk," she said regaining her composure.

Skip, Doug, and Pierce were exhausted, and Corbin Gram and Dr. Butterworth knew they needed to give the three teens some time to unwind.

"Who are the flowers from?" Doug asked, before the three adults could leave.

"Well, perhaps you should read the card," Corbin Gram suggested.

To Doug, Skip, and Pierce

Congratulations on getting the gem.
Sanger Castle School for the gifted is fortunate
to get you in the fall

Love, Mom & Dad Corbin, Mom & Dad Manion

"Well, there's your permission," Corbin Gram said with a smile, knowing that Doug was waiting for consent to attend Sanger Castle in the fall.

"This is going to be awesome," he said to his friends, feeling excited about the future.

"I can't wait to see what courses they offer here," Skip chimed in, sounding very intellectual.

They all fell into the leather couch in their living room as if it had been days since they sat down, which it had.

"This is unbelievable," Pierce said with a satisfied grin on his face.

"I think this may be just the beginning," Skip said to her two friends. Doug and Pierce knew she was right. They rested on their couch, listening to music.

Later that evening, Parker, Skip, and Doug made their way down the hallway toward the dining hall. Valeo, Patricia Skiba, and many others congratulated them along the way.

"Good job," a voice said from behind them.

It was Jian and his sister Mae, they were walking to the dining hall for the celebration.

"Thank you," Doug said in return.

"If we were going to lose, I'm glad it was to someone who captured the Gem of Gicalma," Jian said. Pierce and Skip smiled.

"However, next time we will give you a better match," Jian said competitively.

"We look forward to it," Doug answered, walking to the dining hall doors. Pierce was surprised by Doug's competitiveness. Doug looked over at Pierce with a grin, knowing what he was thinking.

Eisenhut motioned for Doug, Skip, and Pierce to stop before they walked in. "You will go in a different entrance," Eisenhut said, referring to their entrance from a few days earlier.

They walked toward the portrait of Lord Sanger and the wall opened up to the waiting room in its usual way. An open window that looked out over the castle grounds showed the sunlight that lit up the sky. Suddenly, Mammoth, Eisenhut's Hawk, came flying in the window.

"There you are," Eisenhut said fondly to the bird. "I believe you know Mammoth," he said. Skip, Doug, and Pierce nodded their heads.

"I will go in and quiet the crowd. Then I'll introduce you. Please make sure you enter on time," he suggested with a smile.

"Wait," Skip yelled.

Eisenhut turned around and looked at her before he entered the hall.

"Where's Felicia?" she asked.

Eisenhut was a bit embarrassed for forgetting her, and knew he may pay for it later.

"We cannot wait for her," he said quietly holding something back.

The three heroes didn't notice because of the excitement of entering the dining hall. As he walked out of the room, Felicia came fluttering through the window.

"I'm sorry I'm late. I had to get ready," she said fixing her hair.

"You're always late," Eisenhut said smiling.

He turned and winked at her as he walked out of the room and into the dining hall.

"Well yes, anyway. There is something you should know," Felicia said hesitantly.

"What," Doug answered.

"Well, I…uhm…I," Felicia stuttered.

"What is it," Skip said impatiently.

It seemed that there was one last surprise in store for the teens. Over the past few days they had gotten to know Felicia pretty well, but never realized that they actually knew her all along.

Suddenly, Felicia began to change form and grew quite tall. Actually she towered over Doug, Skip, and Pierce. Her face changed a bit, and her gray hair got quite long, as did her nose.

"Mrs. Eisenhut," Pierce said in awe.

Ethel smiled a very warm smile. The kids were speechless.

"I'm sorry," she began. "I couldn't tell you, and we had to make sure you would be all right," she said warmly.

"It all makes sense now," Doug said. "Lord Eisenhut kept winking at you, and you said he should be the one worried about getting in trouble. "And then the lemonade thing," Doug said, laughing as if everything were clearing up for him.

"Are you all right?" Mrs. Eisenhut asked.

"Yes," they all said staring at her oddly.

The feeling of being in a land far away was completely changed the feeling that they were really home.

"I should have known that no one floats as well as you can," Skip said laughing.

As Lord Eisenhut entered the dining hall, the children all became quiet. He clapped his hands twice for those who did not see him enter. Eisenhut had the attention of two hundred children and numerous adults.

"I am very proud today," he began. "Evil tried to take over and we went through some scary moments, but we prevailed. We are now in possession of the Gem of Gicalma, and we have the power we need to open the school this year," he said, being interrupted by the loud applause.

He waited a moment for the clapping and cheering to die down and then continued to speak.

"The school year will begin in September, and you will all receive a letter stating when you can move in. There will be specific directions on how to use the portals, but I'm getting ahead of myself," Lord Eisenhut said, looking as if he were getting a little emotional.

"All of this would not have been possible if it were not for our new gifted friends. We have three…I'm sorry, four people we need to thank for capturing the Gem of Gicalma," he said with a smile hidden under his bushy salt and pepper goatee. "Please allow me to introduce our new heroes. Skip Corbin, Pierce Butterworth, Doug Manion," he said.

"And Felicia," Doug said interrupting Eisenhut.

"And Felicia," Eisenhut said, slowly staring proudly at his very brave wife.

Regardless of who she really was, Felicia did help, and the rest of the students in the crowd didn't need to know her true identity.

All four slowly walked out to the stage, Mrs. Eisenhut transformed back into Felicia for the ceremony. The crowd erupted in applause as the heroes entered the dining hall one by one. Doug could feel his cheeks turning red. Corbin Gram and Pierce's Dad clapped wildly. Eisenhut walked to the podium with three bronze medals in his hands. The crowd was applauding so loud, and for so long, that Eisenhut had to allow them a few minutes to get it out of their systems and calm down.

Excitement rang through the air, and the crowd was clapping

for the three heroes, the gem, and the opportunity to attend the castle in the fall.

After a few more moments, Lord Eisenhut raised his hand to get the crowd to quiet down, which they did. "I hereby award these medals of honor to our three heroes," Eisenhut announced, walking toward Doug, Skip and Pierce, putting the medals around their necks.

"What do you think of my wife?" he said quietly to the three teenagers.

They all smiled as Eisenhut winked at his tiny transformed wife.

Suddenly a small medal appeared in Eisenhut's hand, and he put it around Felicia's tiny neck. All six toes on each of her feet fluttered about with excitement. Doug was dying to ask her why she had six toes when she transformed into a fairy, but was afraid of the answer he might get.

Once again, the crowd erupted into applause. Lord Eisenhut turned toward the crowd, and took a deep breath as if he had something profound to say.

"Let the festivities begin," he announced loudly. His voice boomed from his diaphragm.

Banners dropped from the ceilings, and trays flew through the air carrying food to each child in the dining hall.

The choreography of the trays was impressive. Candy then appeared in the middle of each table and the children began to stuff themselves silly.

The Barons' orchestra appeared out of the wall and music played. Doug began eating quickly.

"Take your time Manion, no one is going to take it away from you," Skip said laughing. Doug turned a new shade of red and looked up at his grandmother, who mouthed the words, "Slow down," with a smile.

The reddened face was not only brought on by embarrassment, but also because he chomped onto Butterworth's Burning Bushel Hot Sauce that was spread all over Doug's sesame noodles. Dr. Butterworth looked down with a devilish grin, knowing what Doug had bitten into.

"I've been perfecting that," he whispered to Corbin Gram.

She in return began laughing quite hard. Hard enough to knock her off her seat that is. In return, Doug did some laughing himself, after making sure she was all right.

The food kept coming, and prizes were dropping from the ceiling. Not serious prizes, but gifts like, kazoos, noisemakers, and bubble gum, called teeth extractors, which really make your teeth disappear....but only for a few minutes.

After everyone was finished eating, the food trays floated around, and each child put their empty plates on top of them. Doug had never eaten so much food in his life, and the same could be said for every child sitting in the dining hall. It was as if the best planned birthday party got out of control, but luckily for the crowd, being out of control was part of the plan.

The tables were cleared and Eisenhut stood up. The crowd went silent in anticipation of the speech Eisenhut was about to give. The adults were impressed with the crowds manners, but the crowd was actually just too tired to applaud anymore.

"As you know, because of our recent acquisition of the gem, we will be a place of education in the fall. We will mix the usual classes you would have had at your former school, with classes you cannot find anywhere else. Well, except in the gifted world, that is. We have decided you need something with which to begin the year," Eisenhut announced vaguely.

Around the three long medieval tables, long brown boxes appeared in front of some children, dropping from the ceiling in front of others.

"Please allow our champions to be the first to open their gifts," Eisenhut politely asked staring down at the new heroes.

Doug, Skip, and Pierce all looked at each other, but only for a moment, because the gift boxes intrigued them. Or, rather, what was in them. All three began to rip open the brown paper wrapping, and look in the attractive maroon box.

"A wand," Doug yelled, his wand in the air.

All of the children ripped open their gifts to see if they received the same gifts. Gold and bronze wands were given to every child.

It never occurred to them that they didn't know how to use them, but they were excited about the… idea…. of learning how to use them. Although they were very long to hold and some of the soon-to-be students were hitting each other with them by accident.

"You'll be needing those for the school year," Eisenhut announced to everyone. "Please make sure you leave them in your suites until you return in a month," Eisenhut commanded.

The crowd gave an, "Aww," with disappointment.

Lord Eisenhut anticipated that groan of displeasure. Doug was excited that he would be attending school with his friends Skip and Pierce again, just in another place. A very magical and wonderful place. Feeling the necklace around his neck, he rubbed it thankfully. He looked at Pierce's necklace around his neck, and knew Skip had her mirror close to her. They had their wands and a few extras as well, like the brand new Intruder Map. The gifts for the gifted. Doug couldn't wait to learn how to use them on a regular basis.

As much fun as he was having, he looked forward to going home for a month to get ready for school. There were other friends to say goodbye to in Waterville, and some relaxing to do before the much-anticipated, but before the difficult school year began. It was going to be hard to explain why all three friends were leaving to go to boarding schools in the fall, with such short notice.

Doug, Skip, and Pierce didn't realize that their parents already took care of the situation. Each parent explained to the various schoolteachers, coaches, and principals that the three were accepted to a prestigious boarding school where Pierce's dad was a professor.

The celebration continued late into the night, and the three worn-out champions longed for their beds. As they tiredly made their way out of the dining hall, they walked down the hallway, staring at the pictures. The covered picture with black cloth still hung on the wall. Doug thought of all the possible adventures that lay ahead, and one of the most important was to find Ali Choukeir.

As they got to the end of the hall, about to turn the corner to head up the spiral staircase, a new picture came into view. And the three kids in it looked very familiar. Doug, Skip, and Pierce stood and gazed at the smiling photo of them receiving their medals. There was a gold frame around it, which looked unique compared to the silver frames that outlined the other photos. Only one other frame was gold, and that one belonged to the picture of Duncan Butterworth, Frank Corbin, and Marlin Manion. For one evening, Doug, Skip, and Pierce felt like they were on top of the world.

Chapter 6.1
Going Home

"WAKE UP YOU LAZY GOOD FOR NOTHING SLEEPYHEADS!" the voice of Sebastian yelled at the top of his mechanical lungs.

"You have got to stop doing that before we come back here," Pierce yelled at the ornery alarm clock.

Although, secretly he was happy to hear the abuse. It was preferred over the thought of seeing Ludicrous Zwevil. During the past few days, Pierce had formed a bond with his alarm clock. It was much like a child forms a bond with a favorite blanket or a Nothing Pillow (the kind of pillow that over the years has fallen to practically nothing).

"I'm sorry Master Butterworth, I was just trying to leave a lasting impression on you both before you leave," Sebastian said apologetically.

"I can't wake up this way anymore. Understand?" Pierce said.

"Yes, Sir," Sebastian agreed.

"Did you call me... Master," Pierce asked with an eyebrow raised enjoying the name.

"Yes, Master. It is what I have to call you out of respect," Sebastian said. Pierce knew he was going to enjoy his time at Sanger Castle.

"Master Doug," Edgar said waking him up.

Doug was already awake because of all the noise that Sebastian made.

195

"Breakfast will be at eight and then you will be leaving by nine," Edgar said, giving Doug his itinerary for the morning.

The three champions met in their common room and got ready for breakfast. They looked around their suite as if to take it all in one more time. Just to make sure it was actually happening

"This is going to be quite an adventure," Skip said to Doug and Pierce.

"It certainly is," Doug agreed.

All three smiled when they saw three sweatshirts lying folded on the leather couch. Pierce ran over to pick one of them up.

"What does it say," Skip asked.

Pierce turned it around so the front of it was showing. Doug and Skip grinned form ear to ear.

Sanger Castle School for the Gifted was written across the chest of the maroon sweatshirts.

"I guess we can't wear those home," Skip said laughing.

Doug and Pierce agreed, so Pierce left the sweatshirts together on the couch, knowing he would be seeing them in less than a month.

A few more moments to take it all in was all they needed, because they missed home, and knew they were going to be spending a lot of time inside when they got back to the castle. They turned and walked out the double doors, leaving the suite behind.

Making their way down the spiral staircase, they looked at all the portraits, and thought of all the adventures they would be having when they returned for the fall semester.

"I wonder what our teachers will be like," Skip thought out loud.

"It's going to be weird. Like starting over again," Pierce commented.

"It will be unlike anything we have ever done before," Doug said.

He looked excited about the prospect of starting a new school, where everyone thought of him as a hero. After all, he was a part of a team that was responsible for the castle becoming a school. It was a thought that made him feel proud.

Skip, Doug, and Pierce walked past their picture on the Wall of Fame, and a few steps later, they walked past the photos of their parents. When they got to the dining hall, it was arranged like it always was for breakfast. Tables fit for three. They got in line in the refectory to get their breakfast and found that they had an overwhelming hunger.

"Take it easy Manion. No one is going to take it away from you," a familiar voice said behind him.

The kids standing around began to giggle at the joke, and Doug felt his face turn red with embarrassment. He didn't even have to turn around to know it was his grandmother.

"Hi Gram," he said.

"Good morning my Dear," she said politely back.

"Excited to get home are you?" she asked with a smile forming on her soft round face.

"I am, I guess," he hesitated.

"What do you mean?" Corbin Gram asked, as they were walking to an empty table.

Skip and Pierce had already made it there and proceeded to eat. They didn't bother waiting for Doug.

"I feel different," Doug said stopping before he sat down.

"Different how?" his grandmother asked.

"I'm not sure. I just feel like things have changed," he said feeling sort of confused.

"Ahh, that's maturity," she said in return. Corbin Gram was very wise.

He gave her a blank look, not knowing fully what she meant. It was hard for him to grasp the reason why one weekend could change him so much.

"Doug, you are different now. You have done big things, but it doesn't mean you have to act different. And it doesn't mean your parents or friends should treat you differently. What makes the three of you so special is how you work as a team, and how you don't put yourselves ahead of anyone else," she said.

"Why don't you just enjoy the moment and finish the summer. And then come back and work hard in the fall. I heard the Science classes are impossible," she said with a smile knowing she would be his professor.

Doug agreed, like he always did with his grandmother, and sat down. It didn't sink in that his grandmother and best friend's father would be his professors.

Dr. Butterworth came over and talked with the three friends.

"Enjoy your trip home. I'll actually be coming there this weekend, and then I have to come back here. We have a lot of work to do," he said.

Corbin Gram frowned a bit.

"You can't come back with us," Doug remembered out loud.

"No," she said softly. "It's the way it has to be," she said. "It will be fine," she said trying to convince herself as well as her grandson.

"I'll be here with Henry and Ethel, and you'll be back in a month," she said to her grandchildren.

Doug and Skip felt bad that their grandmother could never go home again. It was one challenge they couldn't help solve.

"It will pass. And we'll be together again," she said as if she could read their minds.

"Will you miss home?" Doug asked, trying to let her know it wouldn't be the same without her.

"Sanger Castle is my new home. And I'll have some banana bread here for you when you get back," she said knowing it was her grandchildren's favorite. "Enjoy your trip home. It will be the last time this summer you may be able to get here through Toaster Pond," she confided.

"How else will we get back here?" Pierce asked.

"There's more than one way to get here. Don't you worry," Dr. Butterworth said. There was still a lot Pierce, Skip, and Doug had to learn about the mysterious land.

"If there wasn't, how else would all of these children come?" he said.

The professor had a good point. They just hoped that it wouldn't be another mystery they had to solve. It would be nice if life were easier for a few months.

Skip, Doug, and Pierce were finishing up their breakfast, and Lord Eisenhut walked out to the stage. The noise dulled down and the kids all focused their attention on the Lord of Sanger Castle.

"Boys and girls," he began. "I wish you good luck going home today. We will be having three departures this morning."

Doug and Skip looked surprised at each other. Pierce was focused on the announcement.

"Boys and Girls from Ghent Dormitory will be leaving in thirty minutes from your portal in the common area," he announced. "Queensbury Dormitory will be leaving in one hour from the castle gate portal in the back entrance," was Eisenhut's second announcement. "Exodus Dormitory will be leaving in one hour from Toaster Pond," he said. "I wish you all good luck and will see you after the Labor Day holiday to introduce you to your professors." Eisenhut turned and floated off the stage.

"Do you think he does that to be dramatic?" Pierce said.

"No, I do it because I can," Eisenhut said from behind him.

Doug and Skip were embarrassed for Pierce, but Eisenhut just winked and walked away. Doug turned around to make sure the coast was clear.

"How do all of these kids enter Toaster Pond and not come up in Waterville?" he said.

"It's one of the mysteries of Sangerfield," Pierce answered and stood up.

The three friends grabbed their bags and began to exit the dining hall, walking past the pictures like they had numerous times already and would be doing numerous times again. All three were anxious about the water, and excited to get home.

"Here we go," Doug said as they approached Toaster Pond.

"Remember the speech?" Skip asked her two friends.

"How could we forget," they said in return.

Doug waved goodbye to Valeo and Skiba and walked into the pond. The water began to move up around their waists as they walked deeper. The sandy bottom was coming up between their toes and the water felt warm. Suddenly the sand was not within their reach and they knew it was time to go in under their heads. Around the same time, Skip said the poem that she remembered by heart.

"Walk in deeper
Until your knees are wet.
You're on an adventure
You won't forget.
The water flows
Around your chest,
This adventure,
Will be your best.
The water climbs
Above your head.
Your path will go,
Where you have said."

They fell deeper through the water remembering everything that had happened over the past few days. The water rushed by them and over them, and they felt the magic of the pond surround their bodies. Soon they would be floating up to the Toaster Pond they had known for years. The Toaster Pond that lay across Farm Road from the Eisenhut household.

How odd it would be to look at that house again. Would the town ever be the same? Waterville was somehow different now. They were different. Things that were important four days ago were no longer important. They looked into the eyes of someone evil, and knew they would battle her again. Thoughts raced through their minds as fast as the water rushed by their bodies.

All of a sudden the thoughts stopped. And they began to feel their bodies float up toward the surface of the water. Skip looked up, but she could not see the top of the pond yet. Doug and Pierce looked up and searched for the sun, wondering how deep they actually had gone down, just to make their way back up.

How deep was the bottom of Toaster Pond? Was it actually so deep that they went down to another world, or was it just one big dream to escape the depression of Skip and Doug's dying grandmother and separation of Pierce's parents?

Suddenly the sun came into view and they began moving their arms toward the surface of the water. Skip's red head popped out, and then the sandy brown hair of Doug Manion. Last it was the dark wet hair of Pierce Butterworth. When they caught their breath they all looked at each other, realizing that it could not be a dream, or else they were all in it at once.

"Where have you guys been?" voices of long lost friends from four days ago asked.

Brothers, Seth and Frank Alexander looked at the three coming up from the bottom of the pond, waiting for an answer. It was a lot to ask given that the three had just gotten back from a long journey.

"We were..." Skip began.

"Out of town," Doug said smiling.

Frank and Seth just stood staring at them unimpressed with the thought of going out of town with their parents.

"Yeah, we just got back and wanted to go swimming," Pierce said jumping into the conversation.

"Well you missed the big fireworks celebration for Waterville's centennial," Frank said, as he jumped on his bike.

"We saw some of our own," Doug said smiling.

Pierce and Skip giggled at Doug's remark. Fireworks didn't do their adventure justice.

"Well, we have to get home to do some chores," Seth said getting on his bike.

"We'll see you around," Frank said taking off first. Seth followed right behind his big brother.

"I guess it wasn't a dream," Doug said after the brothers rode off.

"No. My dreams are never that good," Pierce said. Skip had to agree. "I'm heading home," Skip said. "I'll talk with you guys tomorrow," she said getting out of the water, drying off with the towel left behind a few days before.

Pierce and Doug got out and dried off with their towels. Hearing a noise across the street, they looked up to see Mrs. Eisenhut and Rufus walking out the screen door.

"How was your trip?" she yelled, although she already knew.

"It was the best trip we ever had," Doug answered her smiling.

"How did you get here so soon?" he asked Ethel.

"I came this morning to beat the rush," she said smiling.

"Rufus missed me. We'll see you soon," she yelled and walked back in the big white house. Ethel felt good to be a part of a team. The three friends took off on their bikes that just happened to be left for them by the pond.

"Uhm," Skip began and then stopped.

"What is it," Pierce asked.

Skip seemed to stop to choose her words carefully. Doug and Pierce waited to hear what she had to say, as all three rode their bikes along Farm Road.

"I…we…that was the best." Skip stuttered.

Doug and Pierce knew what she was trying to say.

"We make a good team, don't we," Doug said a little more profoundly than Skip could muster at the moment.

"Yeah. The best team," Pierce said, and Skip agreed.

The castle had been around for hundreds of years and was never used to it's full potential. Henry Eisenhut had a vision that he could create a new legacy, and the past few days supported that vision. The next few years would be very exciting for everyone involved with Sanger Castle. Although dangerous and deadly outside the immediate castle grounds, it was a magical land that offered much, and the possibilities were endless. Doug, Skip, and Pierce were the new breed coming, and they had great gifts that they hadn't yet realized. Their teamwork and determination was unmatched, and it sent their enemies back home looking to remedy their weaknesses.

Their small farm town of Waterville holds many secrets, and it has more power than any city could ever hold, because it has Toaster Pond.

Last Chapter

The Fall Semester Begins

"It seems we received a letter my Lord," Parker Gardner announced walking into Eisenhut's office.

"Is it good news?" Eisenhut asked, as if he knew what the letter contained without looking at it.

"I didn't open it sir," Parker answered handing the official looking letter to Eisenhut. Parker thought it was better if the Lord opened it.

Suddenly a smile formed on Eisenhut's face. A dimple formed above his salt and pepper goatee.

"What is it, Sir?" Parker asked.

Lord Eisenhut chose his words carefully, as he always did. It was his wife who was the flamboyant one who spoke before she thought.

"It seems that the Priory of the Gifted has given us permission to go ahead with the accreditation process, and they will be visiting in the spring. They want to give us time to get used to the students," he said as he read the letter. "Things are going the way my father wanted them to," he said with a smile.

Parker knew he was witnessing an important moment in the history of Sanger Castle.

"How can you be sure that no one will be able to get the gem?" Parker asked.

"I have a guard named Eucalyptus, and she can be very

convincing," Eisenhut said with a grin.

Later that day, Lord Eisenhut stood up on the stage as all of the students sat at the three medieval tables to eat their welcome dinner. All of them had their suite placements, and were well rested after a month off. All had enjoyed the rest of their summer. The students had three dormitories chosen for them. It was carefully done before the Castle Cup Competition a month earlier. The same Hide-and-Seek competition where Team Hunter Green, with Skip, Doug, and Pierce had won, and went on to capture the Gem of Gicalma.

The dorms were named Ghent, Queensbury, or Exodus. All three names meant something special to Lord Eisenhut. And all three were as different as the Barons who ran them. Doug felt fortunate, because not only was he going to have his cousin Skip and best friend Pierce as suite mates, he also felt fortunate because his resident director was Baron Choukeir, and she was the warmest, most kind, smart and motherly resident director a student could have. Her characteristics were a good thing and outweighed the one subject she taught, History of Magical Creatures. Doug found that topic to be boring, and a complete waste of his time.

However, Doug was happy to find out that the resident director of the House of Ghent was a man named Khalil Flatbottom. Khalil was welcomed back into Sanger Castle, and Lord Eisenhut was extraordinarily happy he was there. Khalil was not only the resident director of the House of Ghent; he was also a Professor of Forest Magic. A topic he was an expert in. Doug found out that Khalil was a top student when he went to school, and a top athlete as well.

Many were excited to be taking classes with two new professors the kids had heard so much about, although the three teens from Waterville knew them well. Professor Corbin would be teaching Herbology. The other one, Dr. Butterworth, was scheduled to teach Physics of the Gifted, and Sangerfield Ecology.

"There is more out there," Skip said one night looking out the magical windows in the Sanger Castle Library.

"There is another world out there," Lord Eisenhut said egging them on to keep them eager about their surroundings.

When Doug, Skip, and Pierce got back to their rooms, they found supplies they would need for classes, and a directory of the professors they would come in contact with. It was going to be an exciting year.

Faculty Directory

Name	Course Information
Lord Henry Eisenhut	Headmaster
Professor Ethel Eisenhut	(Fairy) & History of Flying
Dr. Duncan Butterworth	Sangerfield Ecology Physics of the Gifted
Professor Mary Corbin	Herbology
Baron Jody D. Doha	World Travel of the gifted Symbology
Baroness Patricia Choukeir	History of Magical Creatures
Professor Hassan Choukeir	Castle Archeology
Professor Khalil Flatbottom	Study of Forest Magic
Dr. Mikael Angertonin	Dark Magic
Professor Tripolina Fahlzalot	Introduction to Spells
Dr. Nefertiti Elsasser	History of Gifted Education
Professor Maggie Doyle	Gifted & Non-gifted Politics
Mr. Parker Gardner	Research Assistant/ Sports Program
Professor Ralphaes SmithClysmic	Tarot Card Reading
Professor Anna Quinones–Leigh	Gifted Language Terminology
Professor Gail Virginia Naylor	Genealogy
Professor Rachel Belokopitsky	Foreign Languages
Professor Effie Giacondo	Vocal Music
Dr. Brad Manion	Instruments of the Gifted
Ms. Pauline Herr	Master Librarian
Ms. Linda Elmendorf	Nurse
Professor George Bollock	Art
Dr. John Cordes	Castle Physician

SPECIAL THANKS

There are many people I would like to thank for all they did, before, during and after I wrote Toaster Pond. Without their encouragement this process would have been impossible. Thanks to them, it was a wonderful experience.

They are:

- Doug, Jo, Dana, and Trish for your unlimited time and expertise reading and rereading the book.
- Dr. Alexander Kuklin and DNA Press for the opportunity.
- Mark Stefanowicz for the cover art.
- Marilyn, Carl (My Pitch Partner), Brad, Jeff (The Neighbors), Mary Beth, Bruce, Andrea, and Lauren.
- My family, friends, colleagues and former students (Saint Gregory's, Arlington, Glens Falls, Watervliet). Your support never went unnoticed.
- SCBWI Albany chapter. Thank you for your encouragement.

Be well,
Peter